INNER SPACE

INNER SPACE

A PRACTICAL HANDBOOK FOR YOUR INWARD JOURNEY TO THE HIGHER DIMENSIONS OF THE UNIVERSE

RENJI PANICKER

ISBN 978-93-52019-27-4

Cover design: Ashwini Jadhav
Layout: Hitanshi Shah
Printing: Thomson Press India Ltd.

Published in India (2019) by
CELESTIAL BOOKS
An imprint of
LEADSTART PUBLISHING PVT LTD
Unit 25/26, Building A/1, Wadala (East),
Mumbai 400 037, Maharashtra, INDIA
T + 91 96 99933000 **E** info@leadstartcorp.com
W www.leadstartcorp.com

To

My late father, Prabhakaran Panicker.

My loving mother, Santha Panicker.

My lovely wife, Ashaa.

My ever-supportive brother, Raji.

My darling sister, Poornima.

And my beautiful daughters, Ahladita, Samiksha and Krishna.

About the Author

RENJI PANICKER is a software engineer and entrepreneur. He is General Manager of a robotics start-up in Pune, working in the domain of Artificial Intelligence. He has a strong experimental interest in Hindu philosophy and has been a meditator since he was a teenager. Having journalled his thoughts and insights for a decade, he decided to compile these jottings into a book. *Inner Space* is his first published work.

Renji can be reached at: renji@segito.com

CONTENTS

Author's Note

THE SPIRITUAL JOURNEY CAN BE quite difficult for people with family responsibilities, but I have been blessed with an amazingly supportive family that has stood by me every step of the way.

From childhood, I have always been an introspective thinker, and I approached this subject too, with a wide open mind, in the spirit of scientific curiosity, with the belief that the universe consists of more than what we can perceive with our five senses. It was backed by a stubborn purpose; that if there was something to be found, I would either find it or be proved wrong.

I have prayed in churches. I have undertaken pilgrimages to Sabarimala many times. Sometimes I went in a group, singing *bhajans* and songs. Other times I went alone, sitting in quiet places in prayer. I have visited local temples and sat in meditation. I briefly joined the Osho ashram. I have attended meditation

camps, *satsangs,* watched online videos of various preachers and teachers, all in the spirit of inquiry and learning, without judgement.

I finally rejected the notion of an external entity, an intelligent God who controls our lives and decides our fate for us, and concluded the truth was within us. I became convinced that there is more to life than what we see and experience objectively, that the spiritual quest had to be internal. So I continued my search, but this time the search was within.

It has been a very long journey, but along the way, I had three major experiences that convinced me I was onto something.

The first one was at the age of 22. I had got a job as a teacher at a school in Panchgani. Since I was working as a contract teacher, I did not have all the regular duties of the full-time staff, and so had a lot of time to myself. I was a very private person at the time and did not meditate in public, or discuss meditation with anyone. Once, I was meditating in my room, sitting in the standard cross-legged

position, when all of a sudden I felt myself floating. I could no longer feel my body. In fact, I felt I did not have a body anymore. I was pure consciousness, drifting in an empty space. After some time, I felt an inexplicable fear and then it was over, just as suddenly as it had started. My eyes opened and I was back. This was my first real experience of something divine, and proved to be a turning point in my spiritual quest, the moment I became convinced I was on the right track.

The next one was at 27. I was meditating at home, again in the standard cross-legged position, when all my attention suddenly focussed on the top of my head, and I began to feel intense waves of energy passing up my entire body. I felt concentric circles around the base of my spine, decreasing in diameter as they moved upwards, rippling through my body towards a point at the top of my head. I felt like I was sitting inside a cone filled with waves of energy, pulling me upward. But the direction I refer to as 'up' was not in the familiar sense of

the word. I experienced a sensation of moving in a direction entirely away from this universe.

The third experience was much later in life, when I was 42. It was a long time since my second experience at 27, when I was not married. This third one was when I was married and had three children. By now I had mastered the ability to freely enter a meditative, no-thought state of mind while sitting, lying down, or even walking. I had got into the habit of drifting into sleep by shutting down all thought from the mind. At the time of this experience, I was lying in my bed, about to go to sleep when suddenly I experienced absolute silence all around. The usual ambient noises, like vehicles on the road nearby, fell silent. All I heard was a steady sound, like a waterfall, but more soothing and pleasant. The sound seemed to be coming from within my head but I could not identify a specific direction from where it came.

This experience lasted for a few minutes, after which, even though the ambient sounds returned, the inner sound remained with me,

and it has done ever since to this day, guiding me along my spiritual journey.

I have subsequently had many more similar experiences, but it was these three that showed me I was on the right track.

As I progressed on my journey, I inevitably reached a stage where nothing perturbed me anymore. I carried out all my material responsibilities, doing everything that needed to be done to the best of my abilities, without letting anything or anyone affect my mental and emotional balance. I successfully navigated through an extremely bad phase of life, which saw me dealing with financial troubles, business problems, loss of friends, self-destructive tendencies, and various other issues, but I came out unaffected. I reached a stage where, despite many adverse interactions with people around me, I felt no negativity towards anyone. I only felt gratitude, when people helped me, and when they could not. I felt goodwill towards everyone, even those who had created obstacles in my material life.

It was this difficult phase that gave me the opportunity for intense introspection, about god, myself, and my relationship with my inner divinity. I realised that my problems were the result of my own bad decisions. I also had the momentous realisation that my bad decisions themselves had a purpose in my life – to stress me out just enough to make me question my material desires and turn inward. I began to introspect on questions like: Is there an external Being who put me through a difficult time so I would discover my true Self? Was my difficult phase a series of events which caused me to discover my true identity because I went through it?

At one time I reached a stage where it became easier to enter into meditation. Sure, I had all sorts of material problems, but entering into meditation would feel like I was jumping into water. I floundered around, my mind jumping about. I'd be kicking water (so to speak) for a while. And then I would stabilise and experience an immense calm. So, as a side effect, I found that in addition to self-discovery,

meditation was a big stress reliever. The bigger the problems I faced, the more I would turn to meditation for comfort.

I reached a stage when it felt like I was perpetually on a thin sheet of ice, waiting for the moment when it would break and I would fall through. But it did not happen and I felt frustrated.

My biggest breakthrough came early one morning when I was sitting in meditation. At one point I felt like I had entered a dream state, except I knew I had not because I was simultaneously aware that I was, in fact, meditating. In this heightened state, I 'saw' how a moment of time becomes a larger period of time, how memories get added before and after. Time was not sequential in the manner we are familiar with. It was multiple events unfolding simultaneously, in parallel. I could not only see the beginning and end of the sequence, I could even add or remove events and random moments in the sequence.

When I emerged from meditation, I remembered what I had experienced just as we

remember a dream on waking. But in this case, I had a parallel memory of how the dream sequence was created in my mind. I intuitively had the realisation that not only was this how dreams are formed, but life as we know it as well. I experienced a heady feeling, like I had understood life itself. Have you ever been in a dream where someone is calling your name, and woken up to hear someone actually calling your name? This happens because, after you wake up, your consciousness inserts a false memory of the dream in your brain to make you believe you actually had that dream.

Most religious books speak the language of faith: 'He is everywhere.' 'He can see you, you can't see him.' 'You must merge into him like a river into an ocean.' 'Feel energy within.' 'Raise your kundalini.' 'Open your chakras.' But I had to know more.

As a person from a science background, my biggest obstacle was reconciling spiritual teachings with my scientific learning. I found it difficult to accept anything on faith. At

the same time, I did not want to blindly reject ancient wisdom and practises. So I was constantly in search of logical interpretations of spiritual wisdom. Sometimes I found it, sometimes I didn't, and at times I realised I was wrong.

For example, I could not accept the notion that if I prayed in a temple, I would get something in return from a god who would be pleased by my act of worship. But I could accept that a temple is a quiet place with a spiritual atmosphere, a place where people respect your need for peace and silence and leave you be if they see you sitting with eyes closed. So, to that extent, I concluded this practice originated from times when a temple was the place to go if one was looking for solitude to meditate and gain spiritual realisation.

My approach was to treat all spiritual knowledge available as a proposition that needed to be considered, and if possible, proven. But I soon realised that any proof would necessarily be subjective, an internal experience. This was

when I concluded that it was best not to worry about any scientific validation for the moment, and just focus on making individual progress in this field.

I realised that all the events of my life were subjective experiences, and I had nothing to show for it, absolutely nothing. And then it occurred to me, why bother? Why try to show objective proof to anyone else? What purpose would it serve?

All personal experiences described in this book are true, but like you, I too, am a seeker and a student. I am still awaiting the ultimate experience. Till then, I choose to believe it is there. In this book, I share my experiences with you and hope they help you travel further along your inward journey.

INTRODUCTION

I am not a religious person, but I am spiritual
I don't believe in God, but I believe there is something out there.
My scientific background does not allow me to believe in gods.
Who am I?
What is the purpose of life?

HAVE YOU FELT LIKE THIS at any time in your life? You cannot shake the feeling that there is something more to life than the daily hustle and bustle, yet, as an educated person, you refuse to accept anything on faith, as demanded by most religions. You feel an emptiness in your life, the nagging thought that there has to be something more to life than an existence consisting of eating, sleeping and procreating. You want to turn to spirituality because you want more than this, and seek answers to the larger questions of life, its purpose, its meaning, and your place in the universe. But your education does not let you blindly accept anything on faith.

This book is for you. It explains the reasoning behind human spirituality from a Hindu

perspective and describes how you can be a perfectly normal, rational individual and still hold spiritual beliefs that do not violate your scientific understanding, or require blind devotion. Neither does it require you to suspend critical thought. It tries to describe the higher purpose of human existence rationally and establish that science and spirituality do not have to be a mutually exclusive dichotomy.

I believe Hindu philosophy and present day science are converging towards the same idea – that the universe we live in exists in a larger dimensional universe. I describe this convergence in the first few chapters and, to the best of my knowledge, I believe I am presenting a new perspective. Drawing on my experiences as a trainer, I have tried to convey my ideas and explain concepts in simple language with diagrams, examples and analogies.

With a reasonable understanding of most modern scientific theories surrounding this

concept, I have been reading and accumulating references in Hindu literature such as the *Upanishads,* to support the same. I have documented my findings in this book. It is a compilation of thoughts, observations and experiences I have had in my spiritual journey.

ETYMOLOGY OF THE WORD 'HINDUISM'

The word 'Hindu' or 'Hinduism', does not occur in any of the ancient Indian scriptures. The Greeks referred to the Sindhu River as the Indus, while the Persians referred to it as Hindu, as they were unable to pronounce S. The Arabs referred to it as Al-Hind, or The Land of the Hindus. The -ism suffix was a latter-day English addition, and that is how the word 'Hinduism' came into popular usage.

The traditional term for Hinduism is Sanatana Dharma or Arya Dharma, and its followers are called Sanatani or Aryan. That said, I continue to use Hindu and Hinduism in this book as they are more familiar today.

Getting Started

> A frog lived in a well. It had lived there for a long time. It was born and brought up in that well. One day another frog that lived in the sea came and fell into the well.
>
> "Where are you from?" asked the resident frog.
>
> "I am from the sea," said the visitor.
>
> "The sea! How big is that? Is it as big as my well?" and he took a leap from one side of the well to the other.
>
> "My friend," said the frog of the sea, "how do you compare the sea with your little well?"
>
> Then the frog took another leap and asked, "Is your sea so big?"
>
> "Much, much bigger."
>
> "Well then, nothing can be bigger than my well; this fellow is a liar, so throw him out."

From Swami Vivekananda's speech at the Parliament of World Religions, 15 September 1893

Humankind today is like those frogs in a well. A few frogs, which have managed to climb out and see the world, are trying to tell the others

about the world outside, but the other frogs are unable to comprehend the message.

Different frogs react with different attitudes. Some believe the message and make the attempt to climb out. Others refuse to believe in the existence of a world outside. Yet others want proof that such a world exists outside the well.

Now ask yourself this, which frog are you?

Throughout human history, we have had men and women who tried to tell us about a greater world out there. They faced different reactions from different people, at different times. Some were revered, some killed, sometimes both. The message, however, has always been the same – that there is a heaven 'up there', and there is a God in heaven, and that people too, must somehow find their way there as well.

Some religions had a stronger focus on the concept of God and his characteristics – loving, angry, kind, judgmental, and even male or female. Others were more focused on the concept of heaven, dealing with questions

like: What is heaven? Where is it? How do we get there?

Among the ancient philosophies, Hindu philosophy in particular speaks of not one, but many heavens (called lokas, literally 'worlds' or 'realms'), and downplays the significance of gods. It places greater emphasis on the need to discover heaven, and characterises gods as nothing more than humans who have made that discovery.

Regardless of religion or philosophy, modern humans find it difficult to accept the concept of God or heaven. The biggest obstacle is the idea of 'up there', the place where heaven supposedly exists. From the perspective of modern science, such a place simply cannot, and does not, exist. This book provides a reinterpretation of Hindu philosophy in modern scientific terms, specifically to provide an explanation for the existence of such a place.

In a nutshell, all Hindu texts point to the existence of what we would call in modern scientific language, a higher-order four-

dimensional universe around the universe we inhabit. Just as a sheet of paper is two-dimensional, in a three-dimensional universe, the world we live in, is a three-dimensional universe, which is sustained within a larger four-dimensional universe. If it sounds complicated, the later chapters in this book will provide a simple explanation.

I further argue that the only way to observe this higher universe is by experiencing it subjectively. Our body, mind and intellect are physically incapable of seeing or even visualising the fourth dimension objectively.

Modern scientific methods depend on objective evidence, which is the ability to observe results with instruments, or our senses. But when we set forth on a spiritual journey, we are studying the subject. Here, science, with all due respect, has reached its limitations, and on this journey we need to look at the teachings of Hindu philosophy related to the subjective consciousness of the mind in order to make progress.

This book is not suitable for skeptics; it does not contain absolute proof of anything, just a proposal that is credible and falls within the realm of probability. It does not require blind belief, just a mind open to hypotheses. In this book I have attempted to define our purpose in life.

From childhood, we are taught that our happiness depends on external circumstances, and all human effort should be towards material fulfillment. *I aim to establish that reunification with a higher level of consciousness is not only possible for humans, but also worth pursuing. The aim of all human endeavour should be towards reunifying with our higher consciousness; that is the ultimate goal of human evolution.*

As a person who holds science in high regard, you may attempt to perceive the world around you objectively. You may choose to maintain status quo and refuse to make any attempts to search for a higher purpose, or you can keep searching for proof of its existence. You can go one step further and look at the extensive body of knowledge in Hindu philosophy, interpret it

practically, and set forth on an inward journey of self-discovery. This book describes various techniques by which such an inward journey may be undertaken.

I have made every attempt to comprehensively research the scientific and philosophical topics I have written about. With this book, I hope to move the study of Hindu philosophy from the realm of literature and mythology, to the realm of applied philosophy for inquiring minds. It unabashedly makes comparison between key concepts of Hindu philosophy and science. It takes key Hindu propositions and explains them in modern scientific terms, in simplified language. I also present how you can test the core hypothesis of Hindu philosophy by conducting your own experiments, such as meditation.

Even as a person of pure scientific aptitude you can, through this book, understand and appreciate Hindu philosophy. Whether you are convinced or not, one thing is certain, having read this book, you will look at Hindu philosophical teachings in a new light.

Perspective On Science

Modern science plays a crucial role in improving our material lives. It has improved our ability to travel and communicate. It has helped eradicate disease, cure illnesses, and improved our life span. This science, also known as empirical science, is based on the objective study of the known universe. It is exploratory and experimental, and classifies knowledge into concepts that can be proven, and those that cannot. For example, the statements, 'the earth revolves around the sun' and 'the earth is flat', can both be proved, the former as true and the latter as false. But the statement 'God exists' cannot be proved as either true or false. There is no externally observable evidence, nothing to prove the hypothesis either way.

This is where we hit the outer limits of modern science. But these limits are largely self-imposed. Any scientific method requires that for a hypothesis to be true, it has to be provable, with valid testable and objective observations.

And right there is the first problem – the very definition of 'objective' is questionable.

The Cambridge Dictionary defines 'objective' and 'subjective as follows:

> Objective: Based on real facts and not influenced by personal beliefs or feelings.
>
> Subjective: Influenced by or based on personal beliefs or feelings, rather than on facts.

How many fundamental concepts of science that we believe to be based on facts, would remain valid in a world where people had only four sense organs instead of five? Imagine a world of people blind from birth. Where all living beings in this world, including humans, have never evolved the sense of sight. In such a world, the concept of colour would remain hypothetical, to be theorised and inferred, based on experiments. If a person suddenly developed sight and began talking about the concept of colour to the others, they would not be able to comprehend what he was talking about. They would call it a subjective opinion, merely because he was the only person who could see colour.

In chemistry, there is a solution called the Marquis Reagent, which is a mixture of formaldehyde and sulphuric acid. It is commonly used to test for drugs, which it indicates by a change in colour. When it comes into contact with methamphetamine (a drug commonly known as meth), it changes colour from orange to brown. This is typically how a prosecution lawyer provides evidence in a court that a seized substance is indeed a drug or not. Imagine a world where everyone is blind, where no one can see, but all other senses are exactly as they are today. Now imagine a courtroom in a drug case. How would the prosecution provide conclusive evidence of a substance being a drug?

Another well known test is the litmus paper test for acidity. It is a blue coloured paper which turns red on contact with any acidic substance. Based on the litmus paper test, how would a blind chemist determine whether a substance is acidic?

Hence, objective evidence is not literally objective. It is dependent on, and limited to, the capabilities of the human sensory organs.

What would happen in such a world if a person were to suddenly gain the gift of sight and start proclaiming that he can 'see colours'? No one would believe him. And if they did, he would be treated either as a god, or a mental patient. What if he were to proclaim to a group of people that if they take five steps forward, they would fall off a cliff and die, and it actually happens? The poor fellow would be crucified for witchcraft!

Taking the sightless world example further, how advanced would fields like astronomy be when they depend so heavily on visual inspection of planetary bodies and light emissions, etc? Sure, there would have be advances and progress, scientists would have figured alternate mechanisms for measuring the characteristics of distant light reaching our planet, but it would not be as much as, or as fast as, what we have achieved today.

It is no doubt true that today, most modern astronomical systems and techniques don't rely on raw vision as much as they used to but there

is no denying that modern astronomy is where it is solely because of the initial research done through visual observation.

While science deserves all due respect for improving our material lives, it has no role in an individual's spiritual quest. There is nothing in spiritual study that can be, or even needs to be, objectively demonstrated. Science serves humanity to the extent that it improves our material existence, but to find true meaning and purpose in life, we have to go beyond.

In any case, the spiritual seeker need not see science and spirituality as a mutually exclusive dichotomy. Much of what science speculates on these days, such as consciousness, artificial intelligence, time, quantum mechanics, and so on, falls into the grey area between hard science and philosophy, where the line between the object and the observer is getting increasingly blurred.

The real question a spiritual seeker has to introspect on is: Do we really need a more comfortable life and an increased lifespan

(goals of science), or do we need a more realistic approach towards life and death (goals of spirituality)?

The moment you believe in the existence of 'something' beyond this world, you can no longer rely on scientific methods to provide answers because science itself is based on objective study and material evidence, while spirituality is subjective.

The way forward from this point is introspection and experience, and a conviction that 'the truth is not out there', as Fox Mulder said. The truth is within us, in a vast INNER SPACE that exists inside all of us, waiting to be discovered. A vast inner space that, with time and effort, we can become subjectively aware of.

As mentioned earlier, science certainly deserves all due respect on material matters. But in the spiritual journey, a seeker should de-emphasise the importance of science and scientific validation for anything they learn in their spiritual quest. Indeed, it is possible

to combine existing scientific and spiritual concepts into a credible proposition, which can then become a basis for further thought and experimentation. Such a proposition is what we explore in this book.

1 THE FOURTH DIMENSION PHILOSOPHY

A KEY CONCEPT IN HINDUISM is the existence of higher dimensions in our universe. The Fourth Dimension Philosophy of Hinduism states that:

1. Our universe, which is three-dimensional, is enclosed within a larger, four-dimensional universe.
2. This outer fourth dimension is hidden from human perception due to limitations of the ordinary human senses.
3. It is possible to inwardly transcend our physical senses through a process of meditation and withdrawal, and become aware of this higher dimension.

Note that none of the texts refer to the word dimension specifically, in whichever language they were written. It is the hypothesis in this book that many of the concepts, stories, and imagery in Hindu culture describe what we know today as higher dimensions.

This fourth dimension, as described in Hindu texts, is different from the Multiverse Theory being debated in scientific circles these days. It is important to understand the distinction early on. The Multiverse Theory has become popular in modern culture partly due to movies and TV series such as *Interstellar, Lost, Fringe, 12 Monkeys, Star Trek,* and so on. Such fiction has popularised and mainstreamed the concept of parallel universes as espoused by the Multiverse Theory.

The Multiverse Theory speculates on the existence of alternate universes that exist in parallel to ours, each containing a different version of us. Imagine a sheet of paper as a two-

dimensional universe. Another sheet of paper would then be a different two-dimensional universe existing parallel to the first. This theory claims that there exists many such three-dimensional universes in parallel to the three-dimensional universe we currently live in, each parallel universe a little different from the others.

In contrast, Hindu philosophy postulates the existence of worlds within worlds. Universes not parallel to each other, but within each other. It states that our three-dimensional universe is unique, and that it exists within a larger four-dimensional universe. If you place a sheet of paper within a box, you get a three-

dimensional object (the box) containing a two-dimensional object (the sheet of paper).

Going a step further, if you draw a line on that paper, you get a two-dimensional object (the paper) containing a one-dimensional object (the line).

And finally, if you draw a dot on that line, you get a one-dimensional object (the line) containing a zero-dimensional object (the dot). Thus, we have a zero-dimensional world (the dot) in a one-dimensional world (the line), in a two-dimensional world (the paper), in a three-dimensional world (the box).

Taking another step, we ask: Is it possible that our three-dimensional world exists in a four-dimensional world? If so, what does a four-dimensional object look like? This is the core proposition of Hindu philosophy. It speaks of the existence of other universes, known as *lokas*. For example, we have *Vishnuloka*, also known as *Vaikuntha*. It is not parallel to our universe; instead, it contains our universe within itself.

We now proceed to understand the fourth dimensional universe in greater detail.

FLATLAND

Let's start with a gentle introduction, with a short fictional piece titled *Flatland*, written by Edwin Abbott Abbott in 1884, as a satirical take on the prevalent attitudes towards new ideas, especially new religious ideas. The author was quite possibly an awakened person who was forced to hide his enlightenment from the religiously conservative British society of the day. Instead, he expressed himself through the protagonist of the story. It has had a major influence on my own spiritual journey, giving me one of my first few a-ha moments.

Flatland is the story of a flat two-dimensional universe inhabited by flat, two-dimensional people who are shaped like squares, rectangles, triangles and so on. The following is a brief passage from the beginning of the story, where the author describes this universe.

I call our world Flatland, not because we call it so, but to make its nature clearer to you, my happy readers, who are privileged to live in Space.

Imagine a vast sheet of paper on which straight Lines, Triangles, Squares, Pentagons, Hexagons, and other figures, instead of remaining fixed in their places, move freely about, on or in the surface, but without the power of rising above or sinking below it, very much like shadows - only hard and with luminous edges - and you will then have a pretty correct notion of my country and countrymen. Alas, a few years ago, I should have said "my universe": but now my mind has been opened to higher views of things.

In such a country, you will perceive at once that it is impossible that there should be anything of what you call a "solid" kind; but I dare say you will suppose that we could at least distinguish by sight the Triangles, Squares, and other figures, moving about as I have described them. On the contrary, we could see nothing of the kind, not at least so as to distinguish one figure from another. Nothing was visible, nor could be visible, to us, except Straight Lines; and the necessity of this I will speedily demonstrate.

> Place a penny on the middle of one of your tables in Space; and leaning over it, look down upon it. It will appear a circle.
>
> But now, drawing back to the edge of the table, gradually lower your eye (thus bringing yourself more and more into the condition of the inhabitants of Flatland), and you will find the penny becoming more and more oval to your view; and at last when you have placed your eye exactly on the edge of the table (so that you are, as it were, actually a Flatlander) the penny will then have ceased to appear oval at all, and will have become, so far as you can see, a straight line.
>
> The same thing would happen if you were to treat in the same way a Triangle, or Square, or any other figure cut out of pasteboard. As soon as you look at it with your eye on the edge on the table, you will find that it ceases to appear to you a figure, and that it becomes in appearance a straight line.

Flatland, © Edwin Abbott Abbott (1884)

Flatland is no doubt a work of fiction, but the story gives us a very elaborate and useful visualisation. It is a two-dimensional world, and the inhabitants are two-dimensional

creatures. The story describes how we, the inhabitants of the three-dimensional universe, would see this two-dimensional world. We can then extrapolate that to imagine what our three-dimensional world would look like to someone from the fourth dimension.

To understand this two-dimensional world better, imagine a blank sheet of paper on a table, with a torchlight shining straight down on it. You will see a circle of light on the paper.

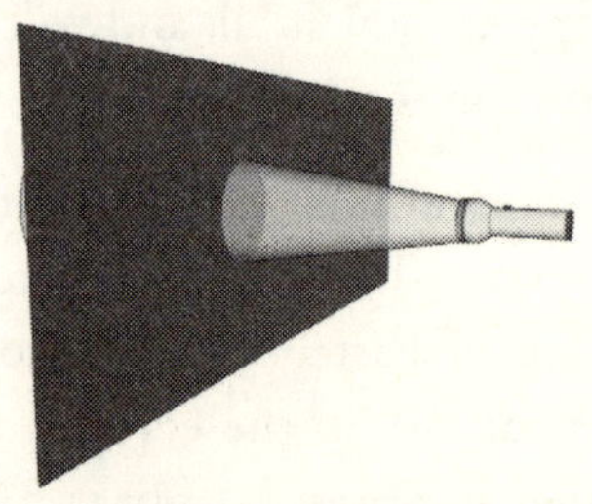

If you shine another torch at the paper, you will see a second circle of light.

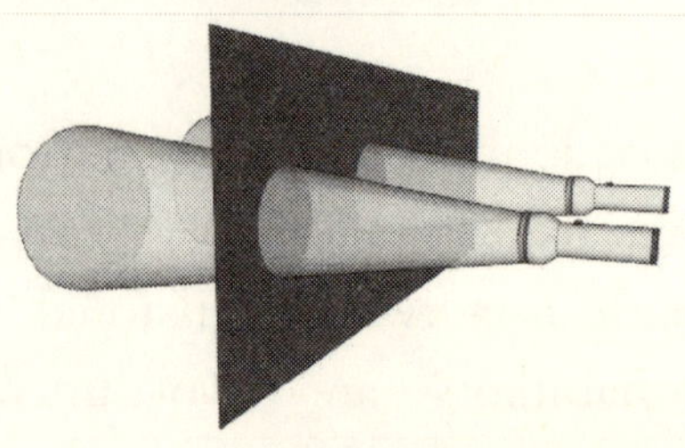

Imagine both these circles of light as living persons. These light-people, let's call them Flatlanders, are aware of only two dimensions. Along one dimension, they can move left or right. Along the other dimension, they can move forward or back.

If they had a third dimension, they would have moved up and down, but they don't have that. They are unaware that such a dimension exists. In fact, they cannot comprehend how it could even exist.

As a result, we can observe the Flatlanders by looking down at them from the third dimension, but they cannot see us because they cannot look 'up'. They can only see other inhabitants of their own world, the other light people. When we observe them, we are doing so from a direction we call 'up'. But the

Flatlanders cannot see us because they have no concept of 'up' or 'down'. They would simply refer to one of the two directions they are already familiar with, perhaps towards one of the edges of the paper. In short, there is no direction they can look towards in order to see us, even though we can see them.

We can now extrapolate this to our universe. We live in a three-dimensional universe where, in addition to left-right and forward-back, we can also move along the third dimension, up-down. Here 'up' generally refers to a direction that points towards the skies and 'down' points towards the ground. If someone were to observe us from a four-dimensional universe, they would be doing so from a direction we have no awareness of, that we cannot perceive. They would be able to observe us but we would not be able to see them.

Most religious texts refer to a heaven which exists 'above' us. But if you are a person who has had a standard education that includes basic math, physics, geometry and maybe some

astronomy, this idea won't sit well with you. Clearly, this place called heaven, if it exists, cannot be in the literal 'up' direction towards the skies, or we would have seen some evidence of it already.

This is the core philosophy of Hinduism. Our universe is a three-dimensional universe enclosed within a larger four-dimensional one. This fourth dimension is the 'up' that scriptures refer to, and it is possible to expand our consciousness to develop a subjective awareness of this larger universe. The rest of this book explains this concept in detail. There is plenty of anecdotal evidence in Hindu philosophy that points to this possibility. There are numerous stories of people who have had a subjective experience of this higher dimension. In order to get a clear visual reference, let's first look at another paragraph from the fictional story, *Flatland*.

In *Flatland*, the main protagonist is a person called Mr. Square. One day, he is visited by a person from the three-dimensional world,

called Mr. Sphere. As you are aware, a square is a flat, two-dimensional shape, while a sphere is a round three-dimensional ball. Mr. Sphere describes his own larger world to Mr. Square, who is unable to comprehend, much less visualise, the third dimension.

> I. Most illustrious Sir, excuse my awkwardness, which arises not from ignorance of the usages of polite society, but from a little surprise and nervousness, consequent on this somewhat unexpected visit. And I beseech you to reveal my indiscretion to no one, and especially not to my Wife. But before your Lordship enters into further communications, would he deign to satisfy the curiosity of one who would gladly know whence his Visitor came?
>
> Stranger. From Space, from Space, Sir; whence else?
> I. Pardon me, my Lord, but is not your Lordship already in Space, your Lordship and his humble servant, even at this moment?
> Stranger. Pooh! what do you know of Space? Define Space.
> I. Space, my Lord, is height and breadth indefinitely prolonged.

> Stranger. Exactly; you see you do not even know what Space is. You think it is of Two Dimensions only; but I have come to announce to you a Third-height, breadth, and length.
> I. Your Lordship is pleased to be merry. We also speak of length and height, or breadth and thickness, thus denoting Two Dimensions by four names.
>
> Stranger. But I mean not only three names, but Three Dimensions.
> I. Would your Lordship indicate or explain to me in what direction is the Third Dimension, unknown to me?
>
> Stranger. I came from it. It is up above and down below.
> I. My Lord means seemingly that it is Northward and Southward.
> Stranger. I mean nothing of the kind. I mean a direction in which you cannot look, because you have no eye in your side.

Flatland, © *Edwin Abbott Abbott (1884)*

This dialogue continues until finally the visitor convinces him of the existence of a three-dimensional universe. The visitor then goes even further to convince him to break out from his two-dimensional world into the outside one.

The following extract describes the experience of Mr. Square as he transcends his world and begins to experience the larger universe.

> An unspeakable horror seized me. There was a darkness; then a dizzy, sickening sensation of sight that was not like seeing; I saw a Line that was no Line; Space that was not Space: I was myself, and not myself. When I could find voice, I shrieked aloud in agony, "Either this is madness or it is Hell." "It is neither," calmly replied the voice of the Sphere, "it is Knowledge; it is Three Dimensions: open your eye once again and try to look steadily."
>
> I looked, and, behold, a new world! There stood before me, visibly incorporate, all that I had before inferred, conjectured, dreamed, of perfect Circular beauty.
>
> ...
>
> Bewildered though I was by my Teacher's enigmatic utterance, I no longer chafed against it, but worshipped him in silent adoration. He continued, with more mildness in his voice. "Distress not yourself if you cannot at first understand the deeper mysteries of Spaceland. By degrees they will dawn upon you. Let us begin by casting back a glance at the region whence you came. Return with me a while to the plains of Flatland, and I

will show you that which you have often reasoned and thought about, but never seen with the sense of sight - a visible angle." "Impossible!" I cried; but, the Sphere leading the way, I followed as if in a dream, till once more his voice arrested me: "Look yonder, and behold your own Pentagonal house, and all its inmates."

I looked below, and saw with my physical eye all that domestic individuality which I had hitherto merely inferred with the understanding. And how poor and shadowy was the inferred conjecture in comparison with the reality which I now beheld! My four Sons calmly asleep in the North-Western rooms, my two orphan Grandsons to the South; the Servants, the Butler, my Daughter, all in their several apartments. Only my affectionate Wife, alarmed by my continued absence, had quitted her room and was roving up and down in the Hall, anxiously awaiting my return. Also the Page, aroused by my cries, had left his room, and under pretext of ascertaining whether I had fallen somewhere in a faint, was prying into the cabinet in my study. All this I could now see, not merely infer; and as we came nearer and nearer, I could discern even the contents of my cabinet, and the two chests of gold and the tablets of which the sphere had made mention.

Flatland, © Edwin Abbott Abbott (1884)

Everything we have read so far describes the bewilderment experienced by Mr. Square when he had to experience a third dimension from his two-dimensional world.

Now, as an inhabitant of a three-dimensional universe, try to visualise the fourth dimension. In which direction does it go? Where does it point? There are three dimensions from you are sitting at this moment. The first dimension is forward-backward, the second is left-right, and the third is up-down. Any direction you look, will necessarily have to be along one of these dimensions.

The problem of visualising the fourth dimension can be easily understood with a simple thought experiment. Look at the corner of a room. You will see three lines converging at a point in the corner. Each of these three lines goes off into one of the three dimensions of our universe, and each has a 90-degree angle with the other lines.

Observe this corner, and think about which direction a fourth line would point if it had to be at 90 degrees to all three existing

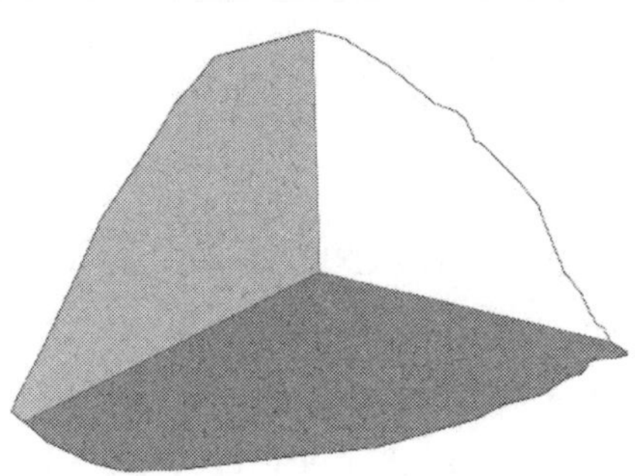

lines. That direction would be the fourth dimension. Sadly, it is impossible to visualise that direction because we humans are creatures of three dimensions. We lack the physical senses and mental capacity to visualise the fourth dimension.

According to Hindu philosophy, we can neither see the fourth dimension with our eyes, nor move in that direction physically. However, all humans have a larger four-dimensional identity that we have lost awareness of over the centuries. If you withdraw into yourself, you will discover that identity within. This inner identity is your four-dimensional identity, and discovering it is the only true purpose of life.

2 Anecdotal Evidence

WHILE MR SQUARE'S EXPERIENCE is a work of fiction presented as an example, in this chapter we will look at descriptions of a few real life experiences of real people, and understand them from the perspective of the fourth dimension philosophy.

Swami Yogananda's Experience

Here we compare Mr Square's fictional work with an excerpt from the non-fictional book, *Autobiography of a Yogi* (1946), wherein Swami Paramahansa Yogananda describes his experience as his consciousness expands from a three-dimensional universe to a larger four-dimensional universe for the first time.

> My body became immovably rooted; breath was drawn out of my lungs as if by some huge magnet. Soul and mind instantly lost their physical bondage, and streamed out like a fluid piercing light from my every pore. The flesh was as though dead, yet in my intense awareness I knew that never

before had I been fully alive. My sense of identity was no longer narrowly confined to a body, but embraced the circumambient atoms. People on distant streets seemed to be moving gently over my own remote periphery. The roots of plants and trees appeared through a dim transparency of the soil; I discerned the inward flow of their sap.

The whole vicinity lay bare before me. My ordinary frontal vision was now changed to a vast spherical sight, simultaneously all-perceptive. Through the back of my head I saw men strolling far down Rai Ghat Road, and noticed also a white cow who was leisurely approaching. When she reached the space in front of the open ashram gate, I observed her with my two physical eyes. As she passed by, behind the brick wall, I saw her clearly still.

All objects within my panoramic gaze trembled and vibrated like quick motion pictures. My body, Master's, the pillared courtyard, the furniture and floor, the trees and sunshine, occasionally became violently agitated, until all melted into a luminescent sea; even as sugar crystals, thrown into a glass of water, dissolve after being shaken. The unifying light alternated with materializations of form, the metamorphoses revealing the law of cause and effect in creation.

> An oceanic joy broke upon calm endless shores of my soul. The Spirit of God, I realized, is exhaustless Bliss; His body is countless tissues of light. A swelling glory within me began to envelop towns, continents, the earth, solar and stellar systems, tenuous nebulae, and floating universes. The entire cosmos, gently luminous, like a city seen afar at night, glimmered within the infinitude of my being. The sharply etched global outlines faded somewhat at the farthest edges; there I could see a mellow radiance, ever-undiminished. It was indescribably subtle; the planetary pictures were formed of a grosser light.

Autobiography of a Yogi, © *Swami Paramahansa Yogananda (1946)*

While *Flatland* describes moving from a two-dimensional world to a three-dimensional world, Swami Yogananda's experience is that of breaking out of the three-dimensional world into a four-dimensional world. The former is something we can easily visualise, but the latter we can only extrapolate.

That difference notwithstanding, note the similarities between this and the excerpt from *Flatland*. For example:

- The similarity in the description of the overwhelming emotions experienced. The two-dimensional person experiences 'an unspeakable horror', while Swami Yogananda experiences 'an oceanic joy'.
- The similarity in the geometric descriptions. If you look at a closed roofless room from one of its sides, you will not be able to see what is inside. But if you look at it from above, you can see what it contains. This was described in the *Flatland* excerpt, where he could see his sons, grandchildren, wife, his butler and others, in their respective rooms. And in the *Autobiography* excerpt, Swami Yogananda describes his experience where he is able to see a white cow on the other side of a brick wall, and people walking down a road that lay behind his head.
- The similarity in the description of the fields of vision. The *Flatlander* describes attaining a circular field of vision. In a two-dimensional world, everyone's field of vision would be one-dimensional. Everything in

this universe would appear as straight lines of varying lengths. Likewise, in a three-dimensional world, everyone has a two-dimensional field of vision, like a movie screen. And extrapolating that, everyone in a four-dimensional world would have a three-dimensional field of vision, such as a sphere.

When a two-dimensional person observes his own world from the third dimension, his field of vision becomes two-dimensional, circular. If we look at the edge of a coin placed on a table, we are not able to see the other side of the coin, or either face of the coin. But if we look down on the coin from above, we can see its overall round shape. This is described in the words of Mr. Square above: 'I looked, and, behold, a new world! There stood before me, visibly incorporate, all that I had before inferred, conjectured, dreamed, of perfect Circular beauty'.

Let's extrapolate this to our three-dimensional universe. When you look directly at a ball, you can only see one half of it, the half that is facing

you. But if you were to look at the ball from the fourth dimension, you would have a spherical field of vision. You would be able to see the entire surface of the ball, from all sides, at the same time. This is what Swami Yogananda describes in his experience: 'My ordinary frontal vision was now changed to a vast spherical sight, simultaneously all-perceptive'.

ARJUNA'S EXPERIENCE

The following extract is from Chapter 11 of the *Bhagwad Gita,* where Arjuna describes (in adulatory prose), what he sees when Krishna gives him transcendental vision, also known as *Divya Drishti.* Using this transcendental vision, Arjuna is able to see the entire three-dimensional universe from an external perspective.

> I see all the gods, O God, in Your body, and (also) hosts of various classes of beings. BRAHMA, the Lord of Creation, seated on the Lotus, all the RISHIS and celestial serpents.
>
> I see Thee of boundless form on every side, with manifold arms, stomachs, mouths and eyes; neither the end, nor the middle, nor also the beginning do

I see; O, Lord of the Universe, O, Cosmic-Form.

I see Thee with Crown, Club, and Discus; a mass of radiance shining everywhere, very hard to look at, all round blazing like burning fire and Sun, and incomprehensible.

You are the Imperishable, the Supreme Being worthy to be known. You are the great treasure-house of this Universe. You are the imperishable Protector of the Eternal DHARMA. In my opinion, You are the Ancient PURUSHA.

I see You without beginning, middle, or end, infinite in power, of endless arms, the sun and moon being Your eyes, the burning fire Your mouth, heating the whole universe with Your radiance.

This experience can be visualised by imagining yourself inside a room. Initially, the whole universe lies outside the room, and you are inside. Then, somehow, the room turns inside out all of a sudden. Your whole known universe is now entirely contained inside that room, and you are on the outside, looking at that universe inside the room. You once thought your universe was infinite, but now you can see it in its entirety, along with its finite outer

boundaries. You are now in an entirely different universe, which is perhaps infinite.

This was Arjuna's experience, and it is explained by the four-dimensional philosophy.

YASHODA'S EXPERIENCE

Shri Krishna's mother, Yashoda, had a similar experience, as described in the *Srimad Bhagwatam*, the life story of Shri Krishna. It happens when Krishna is a child. His friends complain to his mother, that Krishna is eating mud. Krishna denies it. Yashoda asks him to open his mouth so she can check for herself.

> When Kṛṣṇa opened His mouth wide by the order of mother Yaśodā, she saw within His mouth all moving and nonmoving entities, outer space, and all directions, along with mountains, islands, oceans, the surface of the earth, the blowing wind, fire, the moon and the stars. She saw the planetary systems, water, light, air, sky, and creation by transformation of ahaṅkāra. She also saw the senses, the mind, sense perception, and the three qualities goodness, passion and ignorance. She saw the time allotted for the living entities, she saw natural instinct and the reactions of karma, and

she saw desires and different varieties of bodies, moving and nonmoving. Seeing all these aspects of the cosmic manifestation, along with herself and Vṛndāvana-dhāma, she became doubtful and fearful of her son's nature.

[Mother Yaśodā began to argue within herself:] Is this a dream, or is it an illusory creation by the external energy? Has this been manifested by my own intelligence, or is it some mystic power of my child?

Therefore let me surrender unto the Supreme Personality of Godhead and offer my obeisances unto Him, who is beyond the conception of human speculation, the mind, activities, words and arguments, who is the original cause of this cosmic manifestation, by whom the entire cosmos is maintained, and by whom we can conceive of its existence. Let me simply offer my obeisances, for He is beyond my contemplation, speculation and meditation. He is beyond all of my material activities.

Srimad Bhagwatam 10.8.37

This passage uses the act of Krishna opening his mouth as a metaphor for Krishna giving Yashoda a glimpse of the larger universe.

Here, we see a reference to time and the transitionary nature of living beings ('She saw the time allotted for the living entities'). If the entire time duration of a living being can be perceived from an external perspective, it suggests that time itself is a product of the three-dimensional universe. We will discuss the nature of time in more depth later in the book.

Yogi Gopi Krishna's Experience

The next extract is the experience of Yogi Gopi Krishna, when he awakens for the first time. Here, his narration describes the experience of moving out of his physical body.

> Suddenly, with a roar like that of a waterfall, I felt a stream of liquid light entering my brain through the spinal cord.
>
> Entirely unprepared for such a development, I was completely taken by surprise; but regaining my self-control, keeping my mind on the point of concentration. The illumination grew brighter and brighter, the roaring louder, I experienced a rocking sensation and then felt myself slipping out of my body, entirely enveloped in a halo of light. It is impossible to describe the experience accurately.

> I felt the point of consciousness that was myself growing wider surrounded by waves of light. It grew wider and wider, spreading outward while the body, normally the immediate object of its perception, appeared to have receded into the distance until I became entirely unconscious of it. I was now all consciousness without any outline, without any idea of corporeal appendage, without any feeling or sensation coming from the senses, immersed in a sea of light simultaneously conscious and aware at every point, spread out, as it were, in all directions without any barrier or material obstruction.
>
> I was no longer myself, or to be more accurate, no longer as I knew myself to be, a small point of awareness confined to a body, but instead was a vast circle of consciousness in which the body was but a point, bathed in light and in a state of exultation and happiness impossible to describe.

Kundalini: The Evolutionary Energy in Man. © *Yogi Gopi Krishna,* 1937

The above experience can be imagined as follows: Think of a circle with a line passing perpendicular through its centre. This line, the axis, is such that if you take any point on it,

that point is at the same distance from every point on the circumference of the circle.

While the circle itself is a two-dimensional shape, its axis is an extension into the third dimension. In other words, if you are sitting in the centre of a flat two-dimensional circle, and you want to move into the third dimension, you will do so by moving along a line such that you are always at the same distance from every point on the circumference of the circle.

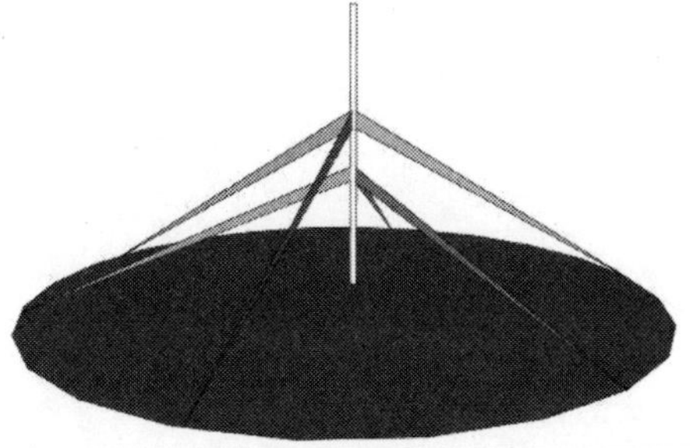

Extrapolating this to the three-dimensional world, visualise yourself floating in the centre of a sphere, a ball perhaps. You want to move along a line that is equidistant from every point on the surface of this sphere. In what direction would you move? That direction is the fourth dimension.

3 Scientific Reinterpretations

IN THIS CHAPTER WE EXAMINE some contemporary scientific theories and reinterpret them from the perspective of the fourth dimension philosophy.

Edge Thickness

Before proceeding, let's think about why our visible three-dimensional universe necessarily has to have a fourth dimension, without which we, the inhabitants, would not be able to perceive each other or any objects within.

Consider this thought experiment. If you hold up a sheet of thick cardboard and look at its edge, you see it as a thick line.

If the sheet was a thin paper, you would see a thin line. No matter how thin the sheet of

paper is, you would always see an edge because the paper always has some thickness. If it had no thickness at all, it would be completely invisible when you look at it edge-wise.

It's the same with the two-dimensional universe. If it was truly two-dimensional, without any third dimension whatsoever, the inhabitants would not be able to perceive each other at all. In order for them to see each other, their universe must necessarily have some thickness, no matter how little.

We can extrapolate this thought experiment to our three-dimensional universe and conclude that it must necessarily have a 'thickness' to project into the fourth dimension. Else, we the inhabitants, would not be able to perceive each other at all.

Atoms and Subatomic Particles

The word 'particle' generally suggests a very small physical object, like a particle of dust. But in Quantum Theory, a particle is

much smaller than an atom, and more like a fluctuation in an energy field, similar to a small wave on a water surface. A particle is not a solid object; on the contrary, solid objects are made up of such particles. Let's understand this with an example.

Imagine an incredibly smooth surface of water. Now imagine a single tiny disturbance on the surface, which causes a small wave to ripple out.

Next, imagine a set of many such waves on the surface, forming a distinct shape. As you can see, we have a set of 15 waves, arranged in the shape of a triangle here.

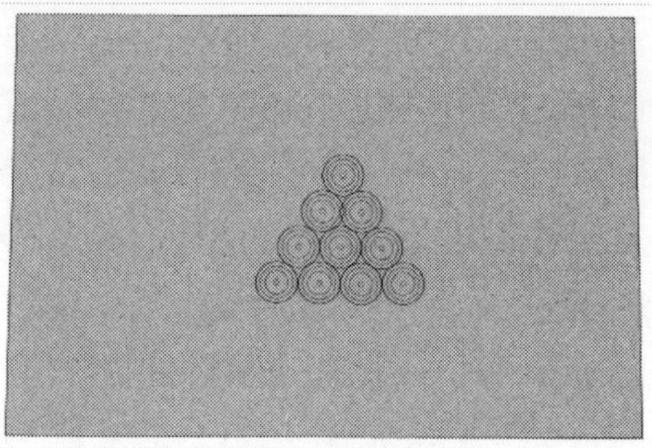

What if we step as far back as possible and then take look at this arrangement? The individual waves are not visible from a distance. All we can see is the broader shape created by them. In this case, a triangle.

And so it is in our physical world. All matter is made up of atoms, and each atom is made of subatomic particles. Each subatomic particle

in turn is not a solid object but a wave in an energy field. If the wave dies down, the particle ceases to exist.

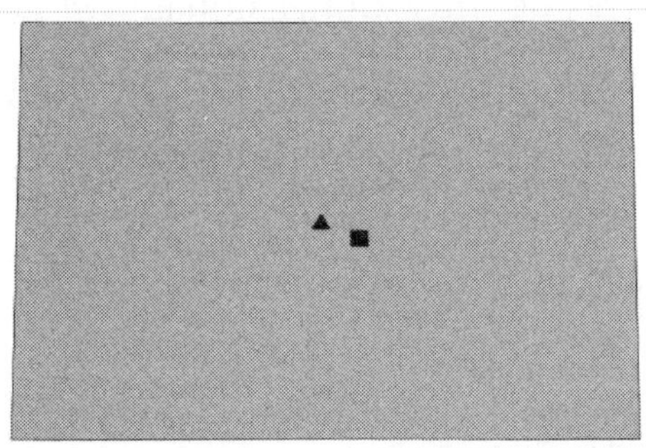

Since we humans are incapable of observing these particles at sub-microscopic scales, they appear as solid objects to us.

We can go a step further and add more shapes to our mental image of this world. We can imagine these two shapes interacting with other, moving closer towards each other, touching, moving away, and so on.

In our current three-dimensional universe, we have observed that when waves are formed on a two-dimensional surface, they are themselves two-dimensional in nature. If we were to

extrapolate this, we can imagine that in a four-dimensional universe, waves would be formed on a three-dimensional 'surface', and would themselves be three-dimensional.

We can visualise a three-dimensional wave as a set of concentric spheres, and understand what physicists mean when they say that a subatomic particle is not a solid object but a waveform.

Electron Cloud

The Electron Cloud Model proposes a theoretical model for the internal structure of the atom. There are many parts of this theory that have been validated through experiments and empirical evidence, but some are still unknown. Here, I propose that a few unknowns can be explained using the four-dimensional philosophy.

Back in senior school, we may have studied the classical model of the atom as proposed by Neils Bohr. That is, round with a nucleus at the centre and electrons orbiting around the nucleus,

like planets around the sun in a solar system. In 1926, an Austrian physicist called Erwin Schrödinger, modified this model to remove the orbits, replacing them with an electron cloud.

In the Electron Cloud Model, instead of the electrons revolving around the nucleus in a fixed orbit, they form a cloud around the nucleus. In this model, the electrons are present at one location when they are first observed. When they are observed a second time, they will have moved to another completely arbitrary and unpredictable location. We still haven't figured out how to calculate that location, where the electron will appear next, or the path it takes to get there.

Bear in mind that Quantum Theory is just a theory and not established fact. But it is currently the most plausible explanation for many observable phenomena in the universe, hence the most widely accepted working theory in the field of science at the moment.

Typically, when you observe a moving object, such as a ball rolling on the floor or a planet

moving in space, you can use its current location, speed and direction to predict where it will be after a specific period of time. For example, such calculations were used by scientists at ISRO, to send the *Mangalyaan* spacecraft to Mars. They were able to calculate how long the spacecraft would take to reach Mars and precisely where Mars would be in that period of time. They could thus calculate the path the spacecraft required to take so the two would meet.

This is known as a deterministic system. It is any system within which we can accurately predict future events using calculations based on current variables. In the above example, the location, speed and direction of the planet and the spacecraft were current variables.

A non-deterministic system, on the other hand, is one where we cannot make such a prediction. For example, tossing a coin. It is impossible to accurately predict whether it will land heads or tails. This is because we do not have all the variables. We have the values for some, such as

initial height, distance from ground, force with which the coin was flipped, etc. But there are other variables for which we don't have accurate measurements, such as force of breeze, if any, in the room, effect of gravity on the coin, etc. And there may be variables we are not even aware of. The combined effect is that we are unable to predict the result of the coin toss.

It is important to re-emphasise that such a system is non-deterministic only because we, the observers, do not have all the variables required. If we did, we would have been able to accurately predict the outcome. So a non-deterministic system is a deterministic system where some of the variables are not known. In such a system, we have to resort to statistics. We calculate the 'probability' of the coin landing heads, and that of the coin landing tails. In this case, there is an equal probability of either outcome, so we say there is a 50% chance the result will be heads, and a 50% chance it will be tails.

With this in mind, let us take a look at a description of the electron cloud.

In 1926, Schrödinger tackled the issue of wave functions and electrons in a series of papers. In addition to describing what would come to be known as the Schrodinger equation, he also used mathematical equations to describe the likelihood of finding an electron in a certain position.

This became the basis of what would come to be known as the Electron Cloud (or quantum mechanical) Model, as well as the Schrodinger equation. Based on quantum theory, the Electron Cloud Model differs from the Bohr Model in that it does not define the exact path of an electron.

Instead, it predicts the likely position of the location of the electron, using what is called a probability function. The probability function describes a cloud-like region where the electron is likely to be found, hence the name. Where the cloud is most dense, the probability of finding the electron is greatest; and where the electron is less likely to be, the cloud is less dense.

Thanks to Schrodinger's work, scientists began to understand that in the realm of quantum mechanics, it was impossible to know the exact position and momentum of an electron at the same time. Regardless of what the observer knows initially about a particle, they can only

> predict its succeeding location or momentum in terms of probabilities.
>
> At no given time will they be able to ascertain either one. In fact, the more they know about the momentum of a particle, the less they will know about its location, and vice versa. This is what is known today as the 'Uncertainty Principle'.

https://www.universetoday.com/38282/electron-cloud-model/

The atom is considered a non-deterministic system, because the location, speed, and direction of the electrons are unknown. This forms the greatest challenge in studying the structure of the atom. We cannot directly see a subatomic particle for it is too small.

Think of it this way: Light is composed of small particles called photons. Usually, we are able to see an object when light, specifically the photons, bounces off it and reaches the retina of the eye. In order to observe an object under a microscope, we need light to bounce off it and enter the eye through the lens of the microscope. But in this case, the object we are looking at is smaller than the photons

themselves, so the photons cannot convey any information about them. If you hold an iron rod in front of a large light beam, the rod will cast a shadow on the wall behind it. But if you hold a strand of hair instead, there won't be any shadow.

One technique used to observe the electron cloud is by hitting it with x-rays and measuring the deflection. When an x-ray hits an electron, it gets deflected, like a billiard ball hitting another. We can now infer the position of the electron from the direction in which the x-ray got deflected.

By doing this repeatedly, we obtain a set of points around the nucleus where we found electrons. This zone is called the electron cloud. So far, all we know is the shape of this cloud. We do not know how an electron moves around within the cloud. Usually, if you see an object at one place, and then you see it at a second place, and then a third, it is possible to infer what path it has taken from the first to the third place.

This measurement technique has an unfortunate consequence. When the x-ray hits the electron and gets deflected, the electron itself also gets knocked out of its own path in the process. So it is impossible to observe an electron without altering the electron's path. So we have no way of measuring how the electron actually moves around the nucleus. Do they revolve like planets? Do they buzz around randomly like bees? Are they twinkling in and out of existence, appearing and disappearing like stars? We do not know.

The current popular belief held by many, including Schrödinger himself, is that the location, speed and direction of the electrons do not follow any fixed or predictable pattern. It is completely random. If you attempt to measure its position, you will not be able to measure its momentum, and vice versa, because in attempting to measure it, you have modified it. This is called the Heisenberg Uncertainty Principle.

Albert Einstein did not agree with this. He believed that if today we cannot predict the

electron, it is because of some unknown variables we are not yet aware of. He famously declared, "God does not play dice," refusing to accept that any natural phenomenon can be truly random. But Schrödinger and Bohr refuted this, claiming there are no hidden variables and the movement of electrons are truly random.

This became known as Einstein's Hidden Variable Theory, and I believe that the fourth dimensional philosophy brings it into the realm of possibility, as explained next.

Cross-Section View

Consider the following thought experiment. We observe an inhabitant of Flatland, our two-dimensional universe. As an experiment, we push a small ball through his universe, in front of him. This would look like pushing a ball through a sheet of paper.

We now attempt to visualise what the Flatlander would see. Bear in mind, since he is aware of only two dimensions, he can only see a cross-section, a very thin slice of the ball as it passes through his world. If you cut a thin circular slice of the ball, and then look at the slice edgewise, you will see what he would see. It would be like looking at a coin's edge. Note that although the Flatlander sees a thin, straight line, but he would still be able to infer the curvature of the line, that is, he can make out that it is not a rigid straight line, but a line that curves way from him. Just like when we look at a ball, we can see only half of its surface, but we can infer that it is a curved surface.

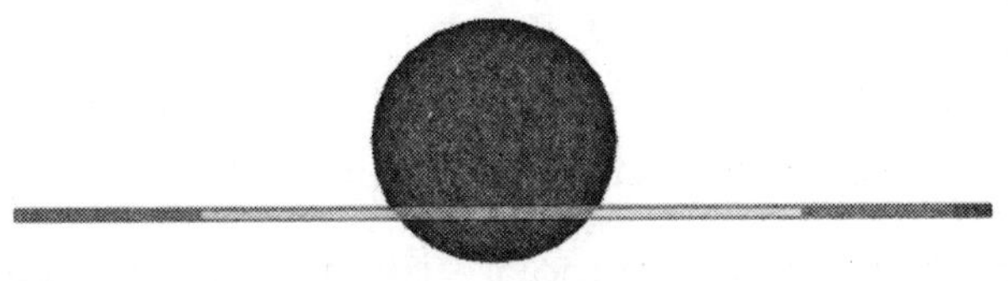

Coming back to the Flatlander, he would be seeing many such circular slices appearing in front of his eyes, one at a time, but gradually.

The first thing he would see is a very small circle suddenly popping into existence in front of his eyes, as the surface of the ball enters his flat universe. He would see this circle suspended, as if by magic, in front of him. This would be like you seeing a small ball suddenly appear in front of your eyes and floating there without any support.

As the ball continues to push through, he would see it gradually expanding in size until we reached the centre of the ball. After that, the circle would start reducing in size until it popped out of existence, right in front of his eyes.

While we are aware of the ball, he is not. So from his perspective, all he can see is a flat circle appearing in front of him, increasing in diameter for a while, then decreasing in diameter until it disappears altogether.

If we were to extrapolate this to our universe, we can envision the experience of watching a four-dimensional object passing through our universe. We would first see a very small spherical object, like a tiny ball, mysteriously popping

into existence in front of our eyes, suspended in the air. This ball would gradually become bigger and bigger like a balloon. After a while, it would start becoming smaller, until it popped out of existence just as mysteriously as it had appeared. Further, if this ball was constantly moving back and forth across our universe, we would not even see the ball. All we would see is a motion blur as it passed through our dimension.

Transitory Subatomic Particles

This proposition states that subatomic particles are physical particles from the fourth dimension transiting through our three-dimensional universe.

To fully understand how an electron cloud relates to the four-dimensional universe philosophy, let us revisit the example of the single wave on a surface. Imagine that wave on a smooth surface as before, but this time, we are observing it from one side. We will see the wave as a curved line of particles, with each particle moving up and down rhythmically.

Let us now imagine ourselves as Flatlanders, viewing the same wave. Remember, a Flatlander we can only perceive two dimensions (forward-backward and left-right), not the up-down dimension.

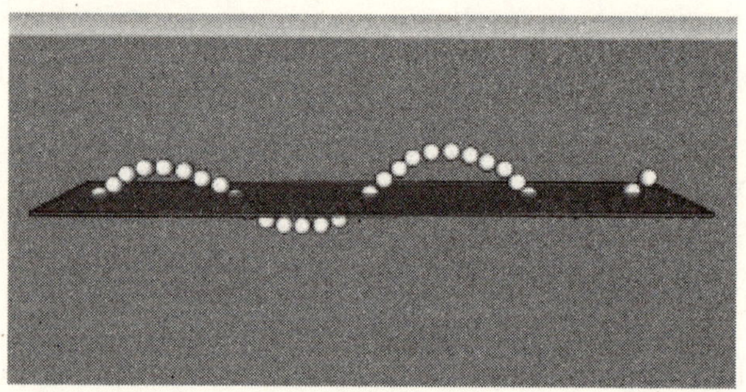

When we, as Flatlanders, look at the wave through the narrow horizontal slit, we cannot see the up-down motion of the particles.

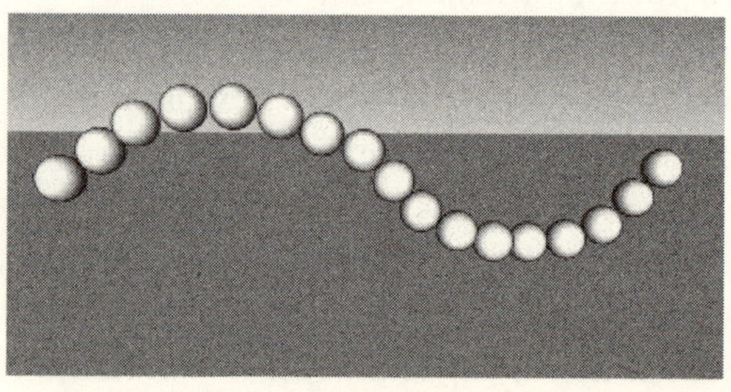

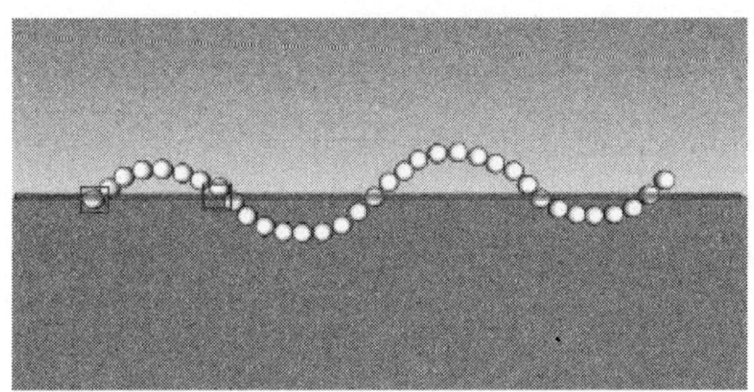

We can only see a small slice of each particle as it goes past the slit, as indicted by the black box in the diagram.

In other words, when we observe a wave on a surface in our three-dimensional universe, we can see the up-down motion of particles as shown above. But when an inhabitant of the two-dimensional universe observes the same wave, he cannot see the up-down motion of the particles. He only sees them appearing and disappearing along a straight line, as they pass through his thin slit-like field of vision.

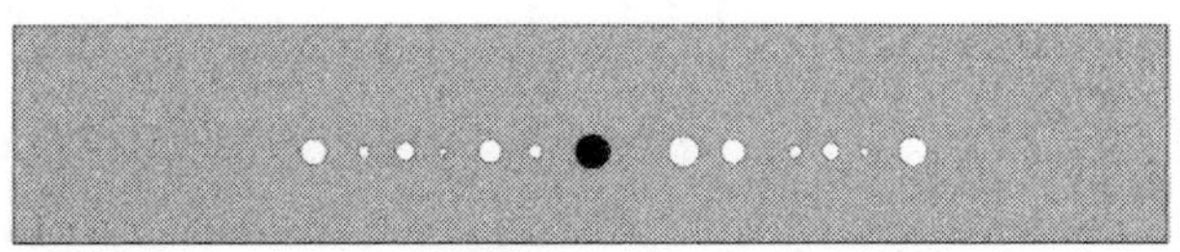

This explanation used a linear wave along a single line as an example. In reality, waves are circular. They originate at a central point and spread outward. If we were to consider a circular wave like in our previous examples, the Flatlander would see the same phenomena, but in a circular shape.

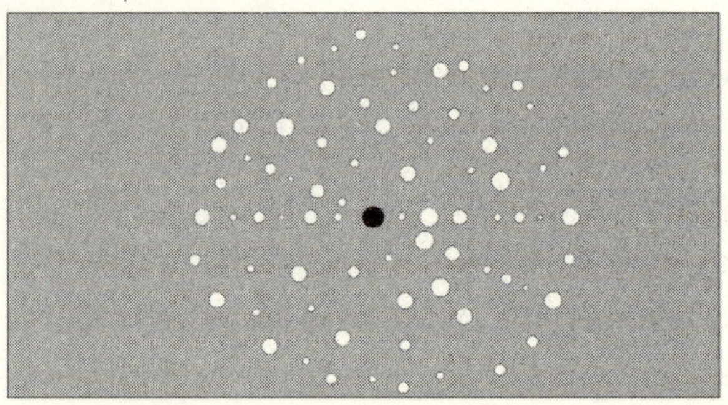

He would see circles appearing as tiny dots. He would see each dot growing larger and larger until it stops growing, and begins to shrink. It keeps shrinking until it disappears. After a while, he would see it appear again, and the process repeat itself. And all these dots would be within a roughly circular area.

Let us extrapolate this observation. If particles of a wave passing through a two-dimensional

plane appear as expanding and contracting circles, the particles of a wave passing through our three-dimensional space would appear as expanding and contracting spheres, within a roughly spherical area.

This corresponds precisely with existing observations of the electron cloud. If electrons are subatomic particles from the fourth dimension space transitioning through our three-dimensional universe, we will not be able to see them in motion, instead we would only see them appearing and disappearing within the electron cloud as they pass through our universe. This would validate Einstein's Hidden Variable Theory, and in turn suggest the possibility that our three-dimensional universe indeed exists within a larger four-dimensional universe.

FALSIFIABILITY: This proposition suggests that quantum physicists are wrong in assuming that the same electron moves from location to location with the electron cloud, that one electron will always occupy one location within

the cloud, appearing and disappearing therein. If it can be demonstrated that the same electron appears at different places within the cloud at different points in time, this proposition will get invalidated.

Virtual Particles

Virtual particles are extremely small particles, many times smaller than the nucleus of an atom. They are capable of gaining and losing mass, apparently out of nowhere.

According to Einstein's Law of Conservation of Energy (e=mc2), the energy within an isolated system must always be the same, it cannot be created or destroyed, although it can change from one form to another.

However, Heisenberg's Uncertainty Principle states there can be very small changes in the amount of energy at a given point in space, for a short period of time, in violation of the law of conservation of energy. That is, for a very brief period of time, the total energy within a very small area of space can go up or down.

This is known as quantum fluctuation and enables the creation of virtual particles. Virtual particles are formed when one subatomic particle splits into two, but strangely the resultant pair of particles are heavier than the original single particle. Although this additional mass is accounted for by Heisenberg's Uncertainty Principle described above, its actual origin is as yet unknown.

Going further, in the early 60s, a physicist called John Wheeler proposed the idea that the universe, when observed at extremely small scales of space and time, is made up of a 'quantum foam' in a state of constant flux, with virtual particles appearing and disappearing from existence, even in an absolute vacuum. This microscopic scale was of the order of 10^-33 centimetres of space and 10^-43 seconds of time (Planck's length and Planck's time).

So, on the one hand, we observe the phenomenon of particles gaining mass apparently out of nowhere before losing it again, and on the other hand, we see how

the fourth dimension philosophy provides a credible explanation for this phenomenon.

Quantum Entanglement

Quantum Entanglement is a very interesting phenomenon. A subatomic particle such as a photon, is split into two using a laser beam. These two photons are then separated across a large distance. When any change is induced in one of them, a reverse change is observed in the other. This happens regardless of the distance between them. It could be the next room or a continent away. In fact, in August 2015, a team led by Anton Zeilinger, a physicist at the University of Vienna, demonstrated quantum entanglement occurring across a distance of 143 kms.

Further, the change in the second particle occurs almost instantly, thousands of times faster than the speed of light.

This phenomenon can be explained by the proposition that the two photons are actually one and the same, appearing at two different

places by moving through the fourth dimension so fast that it appears as two different particles. Bear in mind that subatomic particles are not physical objects, so splitting one does not result in two smaller physical objects. It would be more like splitting a candle flame in two.

Think of it this way: Earlier, we assumed that virtual particles were particles from the four-dimensional universe, passing through our three-dimensional universe. What if these particles are constantly moving back and forth through our universe, like a ball on a rubber string? In that case, if we split the particle into two, the back and forth motion now becomes a circular motion, like the moon moving around the earth.

Now imagine this. If you are standing on one side of the earth, looking at the moon, you see a crater on the left side of the moon. But if you are standing on the other side of the earth, you will see the same crater on the right side of the moon. If you are unaware that it is the same moon on both sides of the earth, you will think they are

two different moons – one with a crater on the left and the other with a crater on the right.

Similarly, it is the same ball cutting through the universe at two different places, but if we make a change to the ball on one side, the same change appears to the ball on the opposite side, because it is the same ball at both places, except that the change is in reverse.

Further, this change is instantaneous, and that can be explained if we assume time is not a dimension but merely a function of our three-dimensional universe. This is explained in detail later in this book, but for now, let us assume that once a particle transcends the three-dimensional universe and enters the four-dimensional one, it no longer follows the rules of time as we know it. If a particle moves from one point to another in our universe, via the fourth dimension, that transition is perceived as instantaneous by us.

Significance of Fire

Suppose we have a two-dimensional world contained within a sheet of paper and we

shine a torch at it so that its beam creates a circle of light on the paper. A resident of the two-dimensional world would see it as a bright blazing circle of pure energy, unaware of its three-dimensional nature. One day, this resident, let's call him Mr Square, breaks free of his two-dimensional world and observes the entire beam of light. He gets into a conversation with the person holding the torch (let's call her Ms. Cube). During the course of this conversation, Ms Cube teaches Mr Square all about light and photons.

Mr Square goes back to his world, thinks over everything he has learnt, and being a scientist, conducts his own series of experiments. One day, he manages to recreate this circle of light within his own two-dimensional universe, without anyone from the higher universe shining a torch at his world. He has discovered fire.

Now something strange happens. This fire, which is in the form of a circle in his two-dimensional world, creates a light beam that travels outwards into the third dimension.

This is now a reversal of the original event. Initially, a beam from a torch created a circle of light in the two-dimensional world, now a circle of light from the two-dimensional world has created a beam that travels into the third dimension.

This beam of light attracts the attention of Ms Cube, who then comes over to visit Mr Square again. He gets very excited by this visit and starts going around his world teaching the other inhabitants how to create a fire, telling them that if they create a fire, they will attract the attention of people from a higher universe.

Similarly, Hinduism gives great importance to the use of fire, or *agni*, in prayer and religious worship. Many Hindu books describe agni as the mouth of the gods, or the gateway to heaven. Agni represents all forms of energy, including life, light, speech, and so on. Agni is closely associated with sacrificial offerings, and many rituals of worship claim that offerings to fire attract the blessings of the gods. Even today, most Hindu weddings, housewarmings,

etc are performed around a fire, into which various offerings are made.

> 1. I praise Agni, the chosen priest, God, minister of sacrifice, The hotar, lavishest of wealth.
>
> 2. Worthy is Agni to be praised by living as by ancient seers. He shall bring hither the Gods.

Rig Veda - I

Note the last sentence that says: 'He shall bring here the Gods'.

The above thought experiment gives us a credible reason for why fire has so much importance in Hinduism and how its importance can be explained using the fourth dimension philosophy.

Consider for example the following passage from the *Katha Upanishad.* For context, Yama, the God of Death is said to know all about the higher world. Nachiketa, a young boy, prays to him and asks him to describe the fire that leads to it.

> I-I-13. O Death, thou knowest the Fire that leads to heaven. Instruct me, who am endowed with faith, about that (Fire) by which those who dwell

in heaven attain immortality. This I choose for my second boon.

I-I-14. I will teach thee well; listen to me and understand, O Nachiketas, I know the Fire that leads to heaven. Know that Fire which is the means for the attainment of heaven and which is the support (of the universe) and located in the cavity.

I-I-15. Death told him of the Fire, the source of the worlds, the sort of bricks (for raising the sacrificial altar), how many, and how (to kindle the fire) and he (Nachiketas) too repeated it as it was told.

I-I-17. Whoso kindles the Nachiketas fire thrice and becomes united with the three and does the three-fold karma, transcends birth and death. Knowing the omniscient one, born of Brahma, bright and adorable, and realizing it, he attains to surpassing peace.

I-I-18. He who, knowing the three (form of brick etc.,), piles up the Nachiketa Fire with this knowledge, throws off the chains of death even before (the body falls off), and rising over grief, rejoices in heaven.

I-I-19. This is the Fire, O Nachiketas, which leads to heaven and which thou hast chosen for the second boon. Of this Fire, people will speak as thine indeed.

Katha Upanishad

Divergence

Our physical bodies, brains and even thoughts are products of the atoms that make up this world. If these building blocks of our universe, atoms and subatomic particles, are not real objects but merely waveforms, or the motion-blur of objects passing through, it stands to reason that our bodies will not be able to move physically into the fourth dimension. It would be like expecting a shadow to rise from the ground. Our physical bodies are constrained by the three-dimensional world. We can only visualise the fourth dimension using thought experiments such as those above.

This is the divergence point, where science and spirituality differ in their approach. A scientist would want to study the fourth dimension objectively, to observe it with the eye, measure it with instruments, form a hypothesis around it, and develop a testable, predictive model around it.

Hinduism, on the other hand, focuses on human consciousness. It makes two claims –

first, that it is impossible to observe and study this larger universe objectively with our sense organs or instruments. And second, that it is impossible to physically move into the fourth-dimensional universe with our material bodies.

The Hindu seeker believes that it can only be studied subjectively, by expanding the consciousness to become aware of higher dimensions, and ultimately 'see' it by reawakening a sense of perception within, that lies dormant in our consciousness.

4 The Hindu Perspective

THE CONCEPT OF GOD HAS EXISTED in almost every culture and civilisation, at almost all times in history. In some cultures, God was a handy explanation for natural phenomena, and in others, God was a convenient means to political ends. Even today, almost all mainstream religions are based on the premise of the existence of an external entity known as God.

Hinduism has been the only notable exception. It is more than a religion; it is an entire philosophical system that deals with the nature of life, sciences, religion, humanity, divinity, and so on. Hindu philosophy even encompasses the nature of atheism in its discourse. It is the only philosophy that speaks of looking within, and has extensively dealt with the subject over centuries, perhaps millennia. It is based on the idea that we ourselves are the divinity that most other religions generally ascribe to an external entity, that every human is God within.

All other philosophical systems of the world, ancient and modern, have only speculated on the nature of the universe and human consciousness, accompanied by theoretical discussion. Hindu philosophy, on the other hand, not only proposes a theory but also a practical mechanism for validating it. It is based on the idea that our three-dimensional universe resides within a larger four-dimensional universe, and every human has a larger identity which has awareness of this outer universe.

It is based on the idea that human beings have lost their awareness of their larger identity, and once we awaken and realise our larger identity, we will gain a subjective awareness of the fourth dimension.

When Hindus pray to their gods, they are worshiping ordinary humans who rediscovered their divine identities. When Hindus meditate, they reach out to their own divinity, within themselves.

The larger four-dimensional universe is known as *Brahmaan,* which transcends the

three-dimensional universe we live in. It is easy to imagine this existing world as the real one and the awakened state of mind as unreal, but in Hindu philosophy, it is the other way around. Hinduism states that this universe is illusory, and defines *maya* as the force that creates the illusion of the world we live in. In a meditative state, you experience the real universe, and what you experience while awake in the world, is illusion.

Hence, people who treat this universe as their only reality are considered ignorant, but that word is not used as a pejorative. In this context, it merely refers to people who are not aware, people who are ignorant of the larger universe and their own larger identity. They are conditioned by their awareness and knowledge of this universe and can never transcend it to know the higher reality. They depend on their sense organs for fulfilment and spend their whole lives attached to their material possessions. This is their material identity, and the life they lead in this world is driven by it.

On the other hand, every human has a soul, known as *aatma*, or the Self. This soul is nothing but our superconsciousness, our awareness of the four-dimensional world. This aatma is our true identity, which we have forgotten. The consciousness that we are currently familiar with, is merely our awareness of the three-dimensional universe we live in. Just as a three-dimensional, cylindrical beam of light makes a circle of light on a sheet of paper when passing through it, our current limited consciousness is formed as a cross-section of our four-dimensional superconsciousness, our aatma.

There are four well-known *mantras,* known as *Mahavakyas* (Great Sayings) in the *Upanishads,* that reaffirm the existence of our individual superconsciousness.

- *Tat twam asi* means 'that is you'.
- *Aham brahmasmi* means 'I am Brahma'.
- *Shivoham* means 'I am Shiva'.
- *Prajnan Brahmaan* means 'Brahmaan is Higher Knowledge'.

The *Mundaka Upanishad* describes this dual identity of humans using the parable of two birds.

> Two birds, inseparable friends, cling to the same tree.
>
> One eats the sweet fruit while the other looks on without eating.
>
> On the same tree a man sits grieving, drowned in sorrow, bewildered, feeling helpless,
>
> But when he sees the second bird content...his grief passes.

Mundaka Upanishad, 3.1.1 - 3.1.2

When you gain experiential knowledge of your aatma, you have discovered a state of existence that goes beyond the material world and the three-dimensional universe. Although your life in the material world itself goes on unchanged, it becomes easier to deal with mundane problems because you have now grown larger than the problems.

Consider this extract from the *Chandogya Upanishad,* for example. In this context, the word dyke (aka levee), means an embankment on the side of a lake or river.

VIII-iv-1: Now, this Atman is the dyke, the embankment for the safety of these worlds. This dyke, neither the day nor the night crosses, nor old age nor death nor sorrow, nor merit nor demerit. All evils turn back from it, for this Brahman-world is free from evil.

VIII-iv-2: Therefore, verily, on reaching this dyke, if one was blind he ceases to be blind; if wounded, he ceases to be wounded, if afflicted- he ceases to be afflicted. Therefore, verily, on reaching this dyke, even night becomes day, for this Brahman-world is ever illumined.

Chandogya Upanishad

Hinduism often talks of the concept of many worlds. The well-known Gayatri Mantra, for example, starts with "Om Bhur Bhuvan Svah". Here, Bhur refers to Bhur Loka, the physical world that we currently live in, Bhuvar is Antariksha, the intermediate world and Svah is the Swar Loka, heaven, the world of the divine consciousness.

The individual aatma, lives in between these worlds, moving from one to the other.

IV-iii-7: 'Which is the self ?' 'This infinite entity (Purusha) that is identified with the intellect and is in the midst of the organs, the (self- effulgent) light within the heart (intellect). Assuming the likeness (of the intellect), it moves between the two worlds; it thinks, as it were, and shakes, as it were. Being identified with dream, it transcends this world – the forms of death (ignorance etc.).'

IV-iii-8: That man, when he is born, or attains a body, is connected with evils (the body and organs); and when he dies, or leaves the body, he discards those evils.

IV-iii-9: That man only two abodes, this and the next world. The dream state, which is the third, is at the junction (of the two). Staying at that junction, he surveys the two abodes, this and the next world.

Brihadaranyaka Upanishad

The *Upanishads* further state that every aatma is part of a larger superconsciousness that exists in this Brahmaan, known as *paramaatman,* the transcendental soul, or the supreme soul. But that's a much higher concept. You need to discover you own higher identity first, only then can you move on to the paramaatma. The aim

of meditation is to first become subjectively aware of our aatma, our Self, and then become aware of the paramatma.

This explains the Hindu concept of reincarnation, the idea that the soul is reborn into this world. The Soul is eternal and everlasting, it never dies. It just moves from body to body.

> III-iv-3: "As a caterpillar, having come to the end of one blade of grass, draws itself together and reaches out for the next, so the Self, having come to the end of one life and dispelled all ignorance, gathers in his faculties and reaches out from the old body to a new"

Brihadaranyaka Upanishad

It is shaped by the general experiences of one lifetime, and get carried on to the next. The specific memories in a life are stored biologically in the neurons and synapses of the brain, but the overall quality of life, the overarching emotions, etc leave their imprint on the soul.

There are two known phenomena that can be explained by this theory of the soul:

1. Prodigies: A person with absolutely no background in music spends all his life learning music until it becomes his life. He becomes consumed by it. In his next birth he is born as a musical prodigy, showing an aptitude for music from an early age, with no training.

   Similarly, a person who is consumed with thoughts of money during the time period leading to his death, will become a money-minded person in his next birth. Likewise, there are people who are fundamentally capable of being happy in life. They always look at the bright side of life; they are always cheerful, and they always try to bring happiness to the people around them wherever they go.

2. Karma: Technically, karma as a system of punishment for a past misdeed, is not a known phenomenon. But the phenomena of bad things happening to a human without an obvious explanation is a known phenomenon, and is explained here as due

> to karma. After you die, you don't go into a world of fire and brimstone, instead you are born back into this world. This next birth is merely an impartial consequence of your activities in this one. If in one birth, a man is unable to intellectually comprehend the idea of the Self, but meditates on it with faith and belief, then in his next birth he is born as a person with greater intellect, capable of greater understanding of the Self. If, on the other hand, one leads a sinful life in one birth, the soul will be reborn either into a lower life form in the next birth, or a human life destined for suffering, and one will have to work one's way back up from there. Over a period of many such rebirths, the soul reaches a level of purity that enables one to transcend this universe and move into the next.

When the soul has unfulfilled desires, it is born again into this world and given an opportunity to either fulfil them, or rise above them. All Hindu scriptures talk about the need to break this cycle of rebirths and achieve liberation (*moksha*).

On a related side-note, astrology deserves a mention here. It is a much-misunderstood and maligned field in Hinduism.

Contrary to popular belief, it has never been about celestial bodies influencing human fate or behaviour. Rather, the position of celestial bodies are used as a measure of time, like the hands of a clock. In a nutshell, astrology says that if you were born at this time and this location, here is a road map for the challenges you will face at different stages in your life.

Ever gone through times in your life when nothing seems to be working out, despite your best efforts? Or conversely, when everything seems to just fall in place? When nothing you do seems to work out? When everything you say comes out wrong and everything you do turns out wrong?

Ever looked at certain people and wondered how lucky they are to have been born into a very rich family, living in the lap of luxury without having to do a single day's work?

Astrology tries to predict your state of mind and intuitive responses to events. Just as when you tell someone "if the clock reads 3:00 am you are probably dull and drowsy", so also astrology says that if the planets are in a certain combination, you will feel a certain way.

Further, destiny and free will are not a dichotomy in Hinduism, they are not mutually exclusive. They are merely two sides of the same coin. Your destiny is defined as the external events that occur in your life, events that are usually outside your control. Events that happen "to you", as it were. The course of these events are usually dictated by factors beyond your control, perhaps the karma you have accumulated in your previous births, but the final outcome of each event depends on how you respond to them. And that response is shaped by your free will. This is, in short, the process by which multiple rebirths lead to spiritual awakening.

Let us understand this further using an example. You are walking across a bridge, and suddenly the bridge collapses while you were on it. There is no way you could have predicted, much less controlled, that event. But now that you are in the water, what happens to you depends on you. It depends on how you choose to exercise your free will. Do you fight, and try to swim for the shore? Can you swim at all? Do you give up and let the water carry you? The event may not be in your control, but the outcome of the event is entirely in your control. It depends on your physical capability and your mental determination to solve your problems and achieve your goals. All astrology tells you is how

> easy or difficult a period of your life will be, it can never predict your response or the final outcome.

Self

It is easy to imagine that this field was documented by a set of people who were able to see our universe from a much higher perspective, the fourth dimension. They possibly were able to see the heavenly bodies as a time keeping mechanism, and make broad statements about the manner in which a soul will respond to various events at various points in time, thus 'predicting' the general quality of that person's life.

Omnipresence of God and Heaven

We are all familiar with religious texts that speak of a heaven that is everywhere, or a God who is everywhere, and who is within all persons and objects. For example, consider this extract:

> III-vii-3: He who inhabits the earth, but is within it, whom the earth does not know, whose body is the earth, and who controls the earth from within, is the Internal Ruler, your own immortal self.

III-vii-4: He who inhabits water, but is within it, whom water does not know, whose body is water, and who controls water from within, is the Internal Ruler, your own immortal self.

...<snip>...

III-vii-22: He who inhabits the intellect, but is within it, whom the intellect does not know, whose body is the intellect, and who controls the intellect from within, is the Internal Ruler, your own immortal self.

III-vii-23: ...He is never seen, but is the Witness; He is never heard, but is the Hearer; He is never thought, but is the Thinker; He is never known, but is the Knower. There is no other witness but Him, no other hearer but Him, no other thinker but Him, no other knower but Him. He is the Internal Ruler, your own immortal self. Everything else but Him is mortal.'

Brihadaranyaka Upanishad

This idea, that heaven is everywhere, can be easily explained by the higher dimension theory.

If we look at a two-dimensional sheet of paper enclosed in a three-dimensional space, we can say that the enclosing space touches every single point

on the surface of the sheet. To explain further, if we shine a beam of light through a sheet of paper, it forms a circle of light on the paper. The beam of light passes through every point in that circle, and we might say that every single point in that circle is 'touching' the beam. Similarly, if the beam of light is absent, we can say that the outer three-dimensional universe is passing through every single point of the surface of the sheet, and in turn, every single point of the surface of the sheet is touching the outer universe.

If you are an enlightened person in a two dimensional universe, you would teach others that it is 'inside' everything in your universe. For example, consider this verse from the *Chandogya Upanishad*:

> That Infinite Fullness, indeed, is below. It is above. It is to the west. It is to the east. It is to the south. It is to the north. It indeed, is all this that exists. Now, with regard to the individual: I, indeed, am below. I am above. I am to the west. I am to the east. I am to the south. I am to the north, l, indeed, am all this that exists.

Chandogya Upanishad VII-25

The other inhabitants of this universe would find it hard to visualise the idea that heaven exists everywhere simultaneously. Likewise, it is hard for us to comprehend the idea that every single atom, molecule and particle in our world 'contains' the higher universe. But it does. More significantly, so does every single neuron in our brain, and this is where our consciousness resides, receiving sensory inputs from, and interacting with, the external world in different ways.

Human Consciousness

Consciousness is a human being's awareness of the world around him. The things we see, hear, taste and feel are all sensory inputs from the world. These inputs ultimately reach our consciousness and we become aware of everything around us. Look at it this way: If the physical body is nothing more than a group of atoms, what makes a human different from a lamp post? It is our consciousness, our awareness of the world, and our ability to think, make conscious decisions and perform actions.

This consciousness is a separate entity from our physical body and mind. We have all experienced the sensation of dizziness for a few seconds. We feel the world spinning around us. We are all aware of the physical cause of dizziness (imbalance in the vestibular system), but that is just the physiology. The real question is: What exactly is spinning when we experience dizziness? It isn't any part of the physical body, for that is completely still. It is our consciousness, our awareness, that feels the world is spinning around us.

However, our consciousness is limited to the three-dimensional universe we live in. The teachings of Hindu philosophy suggest that at some point in the past, humans had the ability to perceive higher dimensions, but over the course of evolution, we lost that ability, for unknown reasons. Hindu writings have alluded to this when they talk of *Kali Yuga*, the Age of Downfall, when humans begin to lose their humanity and values. Kali Yuga is the last of four *yugas* or stages of the world, where vice supersedes virtue

and crime, corruption, superficiality become the norm. The Hindu mathematician Aryabhatta (476-550 AD), calculated the start of this age as February 3012 BC.

If this theory of people losing their higher consciousness is true, then we must ask the question: As humans, did we really evolve? Or have we de-evolved? If the latter, how and why?

There are two possible answers to how it happened:

1. It could be a physical condition. Perhaps we had a physical sense organ associated with the ability to perceive higher dimensions. Hindu texts allude to this as the third eye, usually in the context of Shiva. Perhaps it became obsolete over time, due to disuse, industrialisation, pollution, or lifestyle. If so, it has joined the ranks of other vestigial organs in the human body, such as the appendix, the tail bone, the male nipple and wisdom teeth. Today, our brain can only perceive the three- dimensional world using our eyes and other sense organs.

2. It could be a psychosomatic condition. A psychosomatic illness is a physical illness with mental causes. For example, blood pressure, ulcers, etc are caused by stress. In some extreme cases, people have reportedly suffered from psychosomatic blindness (known as a form of Conversion Disorder), where the patient shows symptoms of blindness without any of the common physical problems associated with blindness, such as damage to the cornea, optic nerve, etc. This condition usually arises from trauma or stress, and requires psychotherapy or psychiatric treatment.

An overall reading of Hindu philosophy suggests the latter possibility, that humans have a 'spiritual blindness' which is psychosomatic in nature; that we once had the ability to connect with our higher nature, but lost it over time. Hinduism claims that this capability is not dead but dormant, and that we have the ability to reawaken it, which would not be possible if it was a physical condition.

As for why this de-evolution happened, the answer is covered in the next section.

Spiritual awakening is the process of reawakening this dormant faculty within us through meditation, and breaking through the limits of perception that constrain us to this three-dimensional universe. Once you do that, there is a whole new universe waiting for you, the promised kingdom of heaven, so to speak.

In this context, we find the word 'know' used extensively in Hindu texts. It has two different meanings. We can know something subjectively or we can know it objectively. When we say 'I know happiness', we are referring to a subjective experience, an internal experience. In effect, we are saying, 'I am experiencing happiness'.

But when we say 'I know Delhi', it is an objective experience, to convey that we are aware of an external object. In this case, a place called Delhi. This distinction is very important whenever we encounter the word 'know' in Hindu texts.

For example, this stanza from the *Kena Upanishad,* tells us that we cannot objectively perceive the higher dimensions.

> I-3. The eye does not reach there, nor speech, nor mind, nor do we know (Its nature). Therefore we don't know how to impart instruction (about It). Distinct indeed is That from the known and distinct from the unknown. Thus have we heard from the ancients who expounded It to us.

Kena Upanishad

We have to experience the higher dimension subjectively. We cannot just observe it with our eyes or other sense organs. We have to 'become' it, not just 'know' about it. This is the real meaning behind the Hindu assertion that the Self is 'beyond knowledge'.

The following stanza from *the Kena Upanishad* describes the subjective nature of human superconsciousness.

> I-1. Wished by whom is the mind directed to fall (on its objects)? Directed by whom does the foremost vital air move? By whom is wished this speech which the people utter? Who is the radiant being that unites the eye and the ear (with their objects)?

I-2. Because He is the ear of the ear, the mind of the mind, the speech of speech, the vital air of the vital air, and the eye of the eye, the wise, freeing themselves (from the identity with the senses) and renouncing the world, become immortal.

Kena Upanishad

Here 'He' refers to the Self within you. This Self, your true identity, is your higher consciousness, which observes the material world through your sense organs. If you are able to transcend the material sense-driven world, you will realise your true identity.

It can be quite difficult to imagine the concept of a trans-dimensional consciousness that is separate from the body, mind, intellect and sense organs, so try the following thought experiment.

As described earlier, if a beam of light passes through a sheet of paper, we see a circle of light on the paper. Here, the beam of light is three-dimensional, while the sheet of paper has two dimensions. So when a three-dimensional object passes through a two-dimensional

object, it generates a two-dimensional cross-section. In this case, a circle.

Extrapolating that, if a four-dimensional object passes through our three-dimensional universe, it would create a three-dimensional cross-section. In this case, a sphere.

Now imagine a small sphere of light, about the size of a marble, somewhere in your body, perhaps within the brain. That ball would be the cross-section of a four-dimensional object intersecting through our universe. The sensory inputs of the body would be hooked into this ball, and your consciousness would be observing the external world from within.

This is superconsciousness, also known as the Self, or aatma in Hinduism. Our ordinary consciousness is a cross-section of this larger superconsciousness, and is responsible for a three-dimensional perception of the universe we live in. But, as a part of the larger aatma, the four-dimensional superconsciousness, it extends into the fouth dimension.

More realistically, the aatma would not be a small ball-like object. The core of the human central nervous system is the brain and spinal cord. Together, they resemble a tadpole, with the brain as the head and the spinal cord as the long tail, both securely encased within the skull and spine respectively. We can imagine this as the intersection, the gateway between the material body and superconsciousness, the aatma. This explains numerous anecdotal evidences in scriptures and recorded history of practitioners of Kundalini Yoga, where they describe the onset of spiritual awakening as a sensation that starts at the base of the spinal cord and travels upwards along the spine, until it hits the roof of the skull, which is when they experience their full spiritual awakening.

Today, we are unaware of our aatma. To be more precise, we used to be aware of it long ago, but over time, we have lost it. We have forgotten our higher identity over centuries of evolution. From this perspective, even though thought and intellectual reasoning are a function of your brain, they can only take you

so far. The seeker necessarily has to go beyond these to proceed further along his journey to reawaken his superconsciousness.

The brain is just another organ of the body, just like, say, the kidneys. The mind is a product of this brain. And just as the kidneys process and purify blood, the mind's job is to process thought. The difference is, we do not identify ourselves with our kidneys. In order to realise our higher identity, we need to treat the mind just as we treat the kidneys. We must ignore it, let it do its job, and cease to identify ourselves with it.

The issue is now whether a faculty for perceiving this higher dimension exists, and if so, how can it be awakened?

For all the progress mankind has made, consciousness is something that has never been, and can never be, objectively perceived, studied, or understood by us. We can only hold theoretical discussions on the nature of consciousness. What happens to it when we sleep, or when we die?

One example of such a theoretical discussion is the well-known debate between Marvin Minsky and Sir Roger Penrose on the predictability of human intelligence.

Marvin Minsky, an artificial intelligence researcher held that human intelligence is very complex but entirely predictable and can be algorithmically replicated. In other words, the sum total of all human behaviour can be replicated by a comprehensive and well-programmed software application.

On the other hand, Sir Roger Penrose claimed that human behaviour is not entirely predictable and hence cannot be replicated by a computer system. In the context of this book, Penrose's position is in line with the subtext of Hindu philosophy.

While Penrose merely stated that human consciousness is 'something' more than the sum total of the biological brain, Hindu philosophy goes on to explain what that 'something' is. It states that human consciousness is a projection of a larger consciousness, from

the larger four-dimensional universe into this three-dimensional universe. It further states that human intelligence is generated from this consciousness.

Unlike science, in the field of spirituality, this claim can only be validated subjectively by awakening a higher sense of perception. A time will come when sufficient numbers of people in various fields, including the sciences, will have awakened to their larger identities. The definition of 'objective' will have expanded to include experiences that we today call subjective. But in the meantime, scientific validation of spiritual concepts has to be kept aside. Till then, our only purpose in life is to discover our true Self within ourselves.

The word 'discover' is a misnomer. We don't really 'discover' or 'find' our higher consciousness, we become one with it. Rather, we become it. This is initially difficult to understand because all our lives we have treated our consciousness as just another attribute of the human body, a product of the brain and the mind, to be

objectively studied and understood. One of the biggest differences between Hindu philosophy and modern science is that the latter considers consciousness a product of the human brain. That is, science believes the mind and body generates human consciousness, whereas Hindu philosophy claims it is the other way around. Hinduism states that the mind, body, and in fact, the entire visible universe, are a product of our consciousness. It describes the whole world as maya, an illusion, and talks of the subjective nature of the spiritual quest.

Going through life trying to be objective about everything is not very different from a zombie or robotic existence. You think, say and do everything logically, but are unable to have subjective experiences that can be achieved only by introverting the mind and looking within. The ultimate state of existence is when we have identified our higher Self within ourselves and subjectively experienced it. It is every human's duty towards themselves to go through an inner process of reawakening and discover their true identity.

EVOLUTION

The obvious question at this stage would be: If it is true that humans have a higher consciousness, why did we lose our awareness of it? Why did people forget their true higher dimensional nature after thousands of years of living and surviving in a three-dimensional world? The answer is evolution. If early humans possessed awareness of the higher Self, the ones that made it through the survival-of-the-fittest process would have been the ones who had greater awareness of the material world. Those whose awareness was concentrated inwards to their higher self, would have had less chance of survival and been eliminated.

As a result, selfishness became an important survival instinct, which in turn gave rise to the ego. This selfishness resulted in humans forgetting their divine nature and focusing on benefits for the material body.

Hinduism actively propounds the theory of evolution, and even describes this process through the *Dashavatara* sequence. Dashavatara

refers to the ten avatars of the god Vishnu, as they appeared on earth. The interesting point to note here is the order of appearance resembles the modern evolution theory.

The Dashavatara sequence is as follows:

1. Matsya, the fish. Symbolises first life on Earth as it appeared in water.
2. Kurma, the turtle: Symbolises the progress of life from water-dwelling to amphibious life.
3. Varaha, the boar: Symbolises the land-dwelling wild animal.
4. Narasimha, half-lion, half-man: Symbolises the mid-stage of evolution of humans from animals.
5. Vamana, the dwarf: Symbolises the short-statured pre-human.
6. Parashurama, the human: Usually shown wielding an axe, represents the early forest-dwelling human that lived off nature.
7. Balarama, the agrarian: Typically shown wielding a plough, symbolises humans who started cultivating their own crops.

8. Shri Rama, the king: Typically shown wielding a bow and arrow, symbolises humans organising themselves into hierarchical, political society.
9. Krishna, the divine: Represents the enlightened human, who has discovered his higher Self, and helps others (represented by Arjuna) to do so as well.
10. Kalki, the destroyer: Shown wielding a sword, symbolises the fallen human who has forgotten his higher Self, and indulges in material pursuits, evil towards his fellow humans, and destruction of the Earth.

Self

This sequence shows the spiritual awakening of humans, and the subsequent loss of higher awareness. Humans, who once had an awareness of their higher consciousness, no longer have it; we have evolved out of it. A person who has had a physical handicap for a very long time will forget he has a handicap over a period of time, and begin to consider his handicapped state as normal. Similarly, we no longer feel the loss, we don't miss it; we can't even accept that we once had a higher identity.

It is our spiritual duty, our sacred *dharma,* to regain this awareness and awaken ourselves to our higher identity.

Time

There are two schools of thought that deal with the nature of time.

1. Time is a dimension. At this moment, we can see or move in three dimensions around us – front or back, left or right, up or down. We can move in either direction along each dimension. According to one school of thought, time itself is also a dimension. That we are constantly moving forward along the time dimension, but without the option of moving backwards. That is, we are always moving into the future one second at a time, but cannot move back in into the past.
2. Time is a function of entropy in our universe. That is, time is nothing but a perception of change. It is only when an object moves from one place to another, do we know that time

has passed, based on that movement. When the needle on the clock moves, we know that one second has passed. Every time the sun rises, we know that one day has passed. If we live in a cave where we cannot see the sun at all, after a while we will lose the ability to keep track of the passage of time. In effect, time is an illusion created by the changes occurring in the universe.

Here's another way to think about it: If our entire universe suddenly came to a complete standstill, where absolutely nothing changes, would the universe still have a concept of time?

It's the second theory that is in line with Hindu philosophy, that time is a function of entropy. Hinduism claims that this universe exists within a larger universe, and then goes on to say that time is a characteristic of our three-dimensional universe; that time is limited to this universe and does not exist outside of it.

The universe we live in is an illusion created, perceived, and sustained by our minds, and time

too, is a similar illusion created by the changes that occur in the universe, changes such as the ticking of a clock or the movement of the sun and the stars. To that extent, Hindu philosophy does not allow for physically moving back or forward in time, much less altering the past or the future.

Hinduism has the most extensive study of time, describing time units and measurements with exact precision, ranging from a millionth of a second to trillions of years. But more important, Hindu philosophy is a strong proponent of the cyclical nature of time, that the three-dimensional universe is repeatedly getting created, sustained and then destroyed.

> The Hindu dharma is the only one of the world's great faiths dedicated to the idea that the Cosmos itself undergoes an immense, indeed an infinite, number of deaths and rebirths. It is the only dharma in which time scales correspond to those of modern scientific cosmology. Its cycles run from our ordinary day and night to a day and night of Brahma, 8.64 billion years long, longer

> than the age of the Earth or the Sun and about half the time since the Big Bang.

Carl Sagan

According to Hinduism, one such cycle lasts for 4.32 billion years and is known as a *kalpa* (aeon), a single day of Brahma. Another such *kalpa* constitutes a single night for Brahma. Thirty such day+night cycles (260 billion years), form a month, and 12 such months (3.11 trillion years), constitutes a year for Brahma. We are currently in the 51st such year of Brahma.

There is a wealth of information on the Hindu system of time measurements in the ancient books, on reading which, we can conclude that the people who wrote them either had an overactive imagination, or had insights into the nature of the universe that can only be had by those who have transcended the limitations of the material universe and physical body.

Books

Hindu scriptures have acknowledged that it is very difficult to explain the concept of

the higher universe. For example, the *Kena Upanishad* stanza I-3 (quoted earlier), describes this challenge as follows.

> I-3. The eye does not reach there, nor speech, nor mind, nor do we know (Its nature). Therefore we don't know how to impart instruction (about It). Distinct indeed is That from the known and distinct from the unknown. Thus have we heard from the ancients who expounded It to us.

Kena Upanishad

Nevertheless, they have attempted to describe the subjective nature of the universe. In the absence of a scientific language, it had to use mythological stories, flowery language, analogies and symbolism to spread the message to the masses. These books are akin to people in a foreign land trying to describe their home country to local residents.

For example, the higher consciousness is described as follows:

> IV-61. As in dream Consciousness vibrates through illusion, as though dual by nature, so in the waking state Consciousness vibrates through illusion as though possessed of dual appearances.

> IV-62. There can be no doubt that the non-dual Consciousness alone appears in dream as though dual. Similarly, in waking state, too, the non-dual Consciousness appears as though dual, undoubtedly.
>
> <...>
>
> IV-66. These (creatures), perceptible to the consciousness of the man in the waking state, have no existence apart from his consciousness. So also, this consciousness of the man in the waking state is admitted to be the object of perception to that man of the waking state alone.

Mandukya Upanishad

Similarly, the symbolic representation of the relationship between body, mind, intellect and Self, described in the *Mahabharata,* is breathtakingly beautiful. Arjuna is the intellect. The chariot is the body, and the five horses are the five sense organs. Krishna, the inner consciousness, is the charioteer, controlling the organs and advising Arjuna on his duty.

The Kauravas are hundred in number, representing all the material joys and temptations the world has to offer. When Arjuna sees the

Kauravas in front of him, he is reluctant to fight them. The analogy here is that he wants to succumb to and enjoy the many pleasures the material world has to offer. He does not want to fight them. Krishna tells him he must. Krishna even shows him the larger universe he can attain if he fights the good fight.

A parallel symbolism exists on the other side of the battle. Dritharashtra representing the mind; he is the father of the Kauravas (material pleasures). He is blind, symbolising the mind which cannot see the bad deeds of his sons. His wife, Gandhari, has vowed to stay blindfolded all her life in solidarity with him. This is symbolic of the intellect, which, despite being aware of the misdeeds of the sons, chooses to ignore them.

Hindu philosophy speaks at length and in great detail, but at this current stage, we will never understand the higher concepts. To use the earlier analogy of the frogs in a well, we are all currently in the well. Once we jump out, we have a whole new wide open world to discover,

but for now, we should work on getting out of the well. Our best approach is to keep our focus limited to breaking through the doors of three-dimensional perception into the higher universe. The rest can wait.

For example, consider this:

> III-xix-1: The Sun is Brahman – this is the teaching. A further explanation is given here. Before creation, this universe was non-existent. Then it became existent. It grew; it turned into an egg; it lay for a period of one year; (and then) it burst open. Of the two halves of that egg-shell, one was of silver, the other of gold.
> III-xix-2: Of these, that which was of silver is this earth. That which was of gold is heaven. That which was the outer membrane is the mountains. That which was the inner membrane is the mist together with the clouds. Those which were the veins are the rivers. That which was the water in the lower belly is the ocean.

Chandogya Upanishad

It would be easy to dismiss this text as religious mumbo-jumbo, or we can suspend disbelief, assume the flowery language describes

something that will become clearer at a later stage, and proceed with reaching the first milestone in the journey. Likewise, with other concepts such as *kundalini, chakras,* etc. That first step is all this book focuses on.

The books on Hindu philosophy cover a vast range of domains – religious rituals, Yoga and postures (*Dhyana-Bindu Upanishad*), Mantras (*Gopala-Tapaniya Upanishad*) and so on. As you may have noted, this book is heavily influenced by the Upanishads, mainly because they espouse and explain the meditative and introspective approach to understanding ourselves. They do not propound any gods or demand blind belief. In fact, one can even see a Vedic influence on some of the later, minor *Upanishads.*

But let me re-emphasise – the Upanishads is just the edge of the ocean. The Hindu body of knowledge in its entirety is very vast and deep, and one should not try to understand it all in your attempt to understand spirituality.

That being said, it is a vague and abstract statement, that probably leaves you wondering what is the vastness I am talking about.

One example is the Upanishads. They are a distillation of ideas found in many other books, written in a manner that is more easily understood by the people. And yet, it is subject to many diferent interpretations and explanations (vyakhyana's). For example, the Kathopanishad tells the tale of Nachiketa and Yamadev, and that tale itself has multiple vyakhyanas. What I have presented in this book is merely one of them.

By way of another more generalized example, I will attempt to describe the vastness of Hinduism's civilizational knowledge, using its approach to epistemology as an example. Epistemology is the science of learning, or the science of gaining knowledge. Put simply, how do you know if something is true, or can be accepted as valid?

In Sanskrit, epistemology is known as Pramana, and there are six documented means of acquiring knowledge. These are:

1. Pratyaksha, or perception. What we perceive/see/hear with our senses. You

gain the knowledge that sugar is sweet because you tasted it for yourself.

2. Anumaana, or inference. You were previously aware that smoke is generated by fire, so when you see smoke, you gain the knowledge that there is a fire.
3. Upamaana, or analogy/comparison. If someone tells you that a saxophone is like a trumpet, but curved, you have gained the knowledge of what a saxophone looks like and will be able to identify a saxophone when you see one in future. This epistemological method is the basis for all human creativity – you look at something as a comparison point and create a new idea. A musician listens to a piece of music and creates a new one that compares to the old one.
4. Arthapatti, or postulation/presumption. If you are aware that your friend is alive, and he is not at his house, then you would reasonably

presume that he is somewhere in the world, outside his house.

5. Anupalabdhi, or non-perception. This is the opposite of pratyaksha. How did you gain the knowledge that your friend is not in his house? Because you went to his house saw that he is not there.
6. Sabda, or testimony. You learn something because you were taught so by a trusted source, for example a person, or a book.

Based on these, India saw many different philosophical systems that were born within the Hindu civilisation. The differences between them lay in which pramanas they subscribed to. For example, Purva Mimansa accepted all six, while the Charvaka school accepted only one, Pratyaksha.

In comparison, Western epistemology had only two documented methodologies.

1. Religious method, which roughly compared to Sabda, and accepted that

certain books and individuals were incontrovertibly correct and their word should be taken as true.

2. Scientific method, which laid emphasis on repeatability and falsifiability. A statement or an experiment is accepted as true if it can be repeated and gives the same results in every repetition. Descartes was said to be the original proponent of this school of thought and is today regarded as the founder of the modern western scientific method. He propounded the idea of doubt, and questioning; that nothing should be taken at face value, that everything should be doubted and questioned, and accepted only if it holds true against all doubts.

This is what I refered to earlier when I said that the scientific method has its limitations. It depends on perception or pratyaksha, but not everything can be modelled as repeatable experiments. If a scientist has a proposition

about how a star is formed, he cannot prove it by creating a star multiple times.

This is where western schools of thought incorporated many of the more sophisticated Hindu epistemological methods like anumaana and arthapatti.

Even the hypothesis proposed in this book about the existence of a 4th dimension universe is an anumaana, an inference – we observe the existence of a 3 dimensional universe and infer the existence of a higher one.

What we are most interested in, however, is the one method not listed anywhere above – Dhyaan, or spirituality, introspection. It is the ability to free-float through various ideas and concepts and gain knowledge subjectively and intuitively, without perception, inference or presumptions. It is a method that makes the experimenter a part of the experiment, and completely contradicts all western scientific methods. This method goes against the Aristotelean logic system which primarily uses deductive reasoning. But it is becoming essential

now and this is why western science in recent times had to graft the concept of dhyaan into their system in the form of quantum logic.

This is just an example of the aforementioned vastness of Hindu scriptures, and the best approach to reading them would be to initially scan them superficially, and then read in depth what appeals to you, skipping the rest. Perhaps you can scan them multiple times, increasing your understanding with each reading.

5 SPIRITUALITY

A PERSON'S SPIRITUALITY IS THE MEASURE of his inclination towards rediscovering his true Self through meditation and other techniques. Some, like monks, dedicate their entire life solely to this quest, while others, not at all. However, the vast majority fall somewhere in between, trying to maintain a healthy balance between their spiritual and material duties.

As a spiritual seeker, your goal in life is to increase your spirituality as you go about your daily life. You cannot reach it by reading about it, or by prayer, or by being a good human being. There is no external activity that can get you there. Most importantly, there is no external intelligent entity who will listen to your prayers and 'grant' you awareness of your higher identity.

You cannot go through life imagining that there is a God who will solve your problems or grant you access to some place called heaven. That

will never happen. There is no one with any discretionary powers to decide your fate. You get what you deserve, not based on what you pray for, but on what you work for. You can listen to or chant all the prayers and mantras in the world, but nothing will happen unless you understand and work towards your goal. You cannot discover your higher Self without going through the effort of introspection and meditation.

The only prayer you need is the constant awareness of your inner self; not the rituals and ceremonies that the word 'prayer' has come to mean today.

The *Bhagwad Gita* says, 'Do your work, do not think of the reward'. Climbing a mountain has its rewards. Perhaps those rewards are what motivated you to start climbing it. But during the climb, when you are just 1000 metres from the peak, your entire body, mind and spirit is concentrated on reaching there. You are not even thinking of reaching there, you are just making the effort. At this time, you are doing your work, not thinking of the rewards.

You must, therefore, perceive it as simple cause-and-effect. The more you meditate on your inner self, the greater the possibility that you will awaken to your higher self. In this respect, meditation is no different from any other effort, such as exercise, sport, memorisation, etc, all of which require constant practice. Except that in those cases, you already know what the result will be. With meditation, you need to know and be convinced that there is, in fact, a reward at the end of it.

On your spiritual journey, you will find people who tell you to forget your problems, or feel them float away, or imagine yourself in a happy place. Unfortunately, it does not work like that when you actually try it. The idea instead is to grow larger than your problems.

For example, imagine working in an office where you are in a state of constant conflict with most of your co-workers. One day, you win a lottery and get lots of money. You decide to continue working there, but now you no longer have the worries you had before. The

people are the same, and their attitude towards you is the same, the problems caused by them are the same, but your attitude towards it all has changed. You are no longer working there because you need to, you are there by choice. If your co-worker or boss troubles you, it becomes easier to walk away. You have become larger than them, so you don't feel bothered by them anymore.

So it is with spirituality. It doesn't solve your problems, but when you become aware of your larger consciousness, your aatma, all material problems become non-issues to you. Everything in your world remains the same, but you feel very differently about them.

During the process of getting to that state, live life as usual, with one exception – as far as possible, keep the mind and thoughts steady on reaching the Self at all times. Remember at all times that the heaven you seek is within you.

The body is the chariot, the intellect is the charioteer, the mind the reins, and the senses the horses. If the chariot (mind) is not controlled,

the horses (senses), become uncontrolled, and you go through life led by your senses, unaware of your own higher consciousness. You search for happiness in the wrong places, looking outward at the material world when you should be looking inward, into yourself.

There is an extremely cliched idea in all religions, old and new, about how we should get in tune with our feelings in order to make spiritual progress. You don't have to actually do that, but understanding the nature of emotions is a very effective way to understand the inner world within ourselves.

First, consider how a human being is similar or different from a machine. Let's take the example of similarity. A thermostat has one or more sensors that detect the ambient temperature in the room and adjusts it. A human being is similar in that he too, is sensitive to heat. He can feel hot in a room and get up to adjust the temperature setting of the AC. In this case, his skin is the sensory organ that detects the temperature of the room.

On the other hand, hearing the roar of a tiger may cause a person to feel fear. There is no sensor in this case. In the earlier example, the skin was a sensor for heat, which was generated from an external source. Similarly, in this case the ear heard a sound that was generated by an external source, but the ear did not generate the fear itself. This primal feeling came from somewhere much deeper within. A machine can never replicate this human reaction accurately. Even if it was somehow possible, a machine could never determine the most appropriate response. Even humans have difficulty with that!

This phenomenon, of humans feeling emotions and generating emotional responses, is a function of the inner consciousness. This is especially true for primal emotions like joy, fear, anger and depression. You have no conscious control over it, neither at the onset nor at cessation.

You will notice that such emotional responses are usually very quick, almost immediate. They take place before the intellect has a chance to

step in and provide a logical rationale for the triggering event. When the intellect does step in, it is much later, when we get the 'why did I do that?' afterthoughts. The instinctive choices you make in the split second define who you fundamentally are. The well-considered actions you take after due thought defines who you want to be.

Consider another example. When you are feeling depressed and want to get away from everything, you look for an escape – alcohol, drugs, a getaway place, a person to talk to, anything. All these mechanisms work by taking your mind off the event that has caused the depression. It is very difficult to come out of emotional states like depression or anger by intellectually rationalising the cause or thinking about it logically.

When your friend is feeling angry about some situation, you speak to him logically and make rational arguments to help him deal with the situation. You are there to ensure he does not take any rash action. But when you are yourself

angry about an identical situation, it is very difficult to apply the same logical arguments to yourself. The difference is that you are feeling the emotion yourself, and you are driven by that emotion.

This phenomenon points to the possibility that emotions are a product of an inner consciousness, and emotional responses originate from a place much deeper within us, more primal than the brain.

When you turn to meditation in order to deal with such situations, it is easy to tell yourself you need to calm the mind. Breath in, breath out, feel your worries leave as you exhale, be content with what you have, and so on. But that's easier said than done because your emotions are being felt by you at a place much deeper than the logical brain. It is even easier to tell others to do all this because you are not feeling what they are. The greatest difficulty lies in actually doing it yourself.

The external world is one that you experience with your senses. You see, hear, feel, smell and

taste it. The internal world, on the other hand, is one that you experience subjectively, through a process of meditation that involves getting the breath, mind and thought under control.

The human being is considered to have four layers – the body, the mind, the intellect and the Self. Your identity, which you refer to as 'I', is not your body, not even the mind, or even your intellect. It is something beyond all of these. The Self, the aatma, the soul, is pure consciousness, devoid of any physical traits. It perceives and interacts with the external world through the intellect, mind and body. The purpose of meditation is to awaken your true self and realise this identity, this consciousness, this aatma, within you.

The aatma is ever free. When your higher consciousness identifies itself with the material world (body, mind, intellect), it gets caught up in worldly matters, hence bondage ensues.

In order to realise your true identity, you have to transcend the body (the distraction caused by the need for physical pleasures and other

sensory desires), the mind (the distraction caused by mental agitations, emotional desires), and the intellect (the distraction caused by analysis, critiques and discussions).

NATURE OF THE SENSES

In order to understand how to withdraw the senses from the material world, we must first understand the nature of the senses themselves. We have five basic sense organs – eyes to see, ears to hear, nose to smell, tongue to taste and skin to feel. We lead a complete worldly, material existence using just these five sense organs. In Sanskrit, these are known as the *Panch Jyanendriya. Panch* means 'five', and *Jyan* means 'knowledge' *Indriya* means organ or senses. These are the five senses of knowledge, with which we attain full awareness of the world around us.

Just as a computer has input devices such as a keyboard and mouse, it also has output devices, such as a monitor, speakers, or printers. Similarly, just as we have five senses for input (that is, knowledge), we also have five

senses for action (that is, output). These five senses for action are two feet (counted as one), to move, two hands (also counted as one) to perform activities, the organ for reproduction, the organ for elimination, and the voice box. These are known as *Karmendriya* in Sanskrit. Here, *karm* means 'action'.

To understand the significance of these 10 organs, let us take a look at a thought experiment, popularly known as the Brain in a Vat experiment.

> It outlines a scenario in which a mad scientist, machine, or other entity, might remove a person's brain from the body, suspend it in a vat of life-sustaining liquid, and connect its neurons by wires to a supercomputer, which would provide it with electrical impulses identical to those the brain normally receives. The computer would then be simulating reality (including appropriate responses to the brain's own output), and the 'disembodied' brain would continue to have perfectly normal conscious experiences, such as those of a person with an embodied brain, without these being related to objects or events in the real world.

Wikipedia

In a regular human being, all sense organs are connected to the brain via a network of nerves. The five organs of the senses feed awareness of the world to the brain, while the five organs of action receive commands from the brain. The brain receives input from the five senses, and commands the five organs of action to act. For example, the eyes see a glass of water and passes on this information to the brain. The brain processes the information and commands the legs to walk towards the water, and the hands to pick it up.

In this hypothetical experiment, the brain is removed from a human and hooked to a supercomputer. This supercomputer is connected to the brain at the precise points where the sense organs were earlier connected, and can send the same information to the brain as the sensory organs used to do. As a result, even though the brain is now in a jar, it continues to believe it is in a physical body with eyes, ears, hands and legs.

Now, if the supercomputer sends a signal to the brain identical to what the eyes would have

sent, there is no way the brain would know the difference. It would believe there really was a glass of water present in front of the body it apparently still has. So, when it sends a command to the legs to move towards the glass of water, that command is intercepted by the supercomputer, and it sends fresh signals to the eyes, to make the brain believe the body is walking towards the glass of water. When the brain commands the hands to pick the glass up to drink the water, the supercomputer simulates the entire experience of drinking the water, including the taste of the water and the feeling of thirst relief.

In such a scenario, would the brain ever figure out that it is not actually connected to a physical body? As you ponder over this question, you will realise the importance of the sense organs, which act as the sole channel for two-way communication between the brain and the external world.

The senses are controlled by the mind, which in turn, is controlled by the intellect. Beyond

the intellect lies the consciousness. We cannot perceive that consciousness using our senses, because it exists deep within us, deeper than where our senses can go.

> I-II-22. The intelligent one having known the Self to be bodiless in (all) bodies, to be firmly seated in things that are perishable, and to be great and all-pervading, does not grieve.
>
> I-II-23. The Self cannot be attained by the study of the Vedas, not by intelligence nor by much hearing. Only by him who seeks to know the Self can It be attained. To him the Self reveals Its own nature.
>
> I-II-24. None who has not refrained from bad conduct, whose senses are not under restraint, whose mind is not collected or who does not preserve a tranquil mind, can attain this Self through knowledge.
>
> 2-III-9. His form does not stand within the scope of vision; none beholds Him with the eye. By the intellect restraining the mind, and through meditation is He revealed. Those who know this become immortal.

2-III-10. When the five senses of knowledge are at rest together with the mind, and the intellect is not active, that state they call the highest.

2-III-11. That steady restraint over the senses they regard as yoga. Then one becomes vigilant, for yoga can indeed originate (in one) and can be lost (as well).

2-III-12. Not by speech, not by mind, not by the eye can It be attained. Except in the case of one who says, 'It exists', how can It be known to anyone else?

2-III-13. The Self should be apprehended as existing and also as It really is. Of these two (aspects), to him who knows It to exist, Its true nature is revealed.

2-III-14. When all longings that are in the heart vanish, then a mortal becomes immortal and attains Brahman here.

2-III-15. When all the knots of the heart are cut asunder here, then a mortal becomes immortal. Only this much is the instruction.

Katha Upanishad

The only way to gain awareness of our higher self is through meditation. We have to calm

our senses, our mind and our intellect, and transcend all of them in order to awaken our higher consciousness.

> I-III-3. Know the Self to be the master of the chariot, and the body to be the chariot. Know the intellect to be the charioteer, and the mind to be the reins.
> I-III-4. The senses they speak of as the horses; the objects within their view, the way. When the Self is yoked with the mind and the senses, the wise call It the enjoyer.
> I-III-5. But whoso is devoid of discrimination and is possessed of a mind ever uncollected – his senses are uncontrollable like the vicious horses of a driver.
> I-III-6. But whoso is discriminative and possessed of a mind ever collected – his senses are controllable like the good horses of a driver.
> I-III-7. But whoso is devoid of a discriminating intellect, possessed of an unrestrained mind and is ever impure, does not attain that goal, but goes to samsara.
> I-III-8. But whoso is possessed of a discriminating intellect and a restrained mind, and is ever pure, attains that goal from which he is not born again.

> I-III-9. But the man who has as discriminating an intellect as his driver, and a controlled-mind as the reins, reaches the end of the path – that supreme state of Vishnu.

Katha Upanishad

Spiritual Journey

Your spiritual journey should be not be about the afterlife, but what you can do in this life. At a high level, there are two possible approaches you can take to spiritual awakening – the intellectual approach, or the practical approach.

The intellectual approach is when you understand the theory and then go through the practicals with the precise knowledge of what the goal is.

The other approach is to directly go through the practical exercises and reach the goal, just as you can go to a gym and perform exercises under an experienced trainer and still lose weight, without knowing the theory behind it.

The intellectual approach works for intellectual people, who have a scientific bent

of mind. These are the people whose minds are constantly ticking. They will not only want to understand the reasons, but also apply critical analysis to anything they learn.

The practical approach works for creative people, who have the ability to keep their mind focussed on a topic for varying periods of time.

Intelligent people love learning, as they rightly should. But there can be no spiritual progress through learning alone. The ultimate aim of spirituality is enlightenment, and that requires practical experimentation.

The following extract from the *Chandogya Upanishad,* where Narada approaches the Sage Sanatkumara for advanced lessons, explains the appropriate learning attitude one must adopt.

> VII-i-I: Om. 'Revered sir, teach me,' thus saying Narada approached Sanatkumara. Sanatkumara said to him, 'What you already know, declaring that to me, be my disciple. What is beyond that I shall tell you.' Narada said:

VII-i-2: 'Revered sir, I know the Rig-Veda, the Yajur-Veda, the Sama-Veda and the Atharvanas the fourth, the Itihasa-Purana as the fifth, grammar, the rules for the worship of the ancestors, mathematics, the science of portents, the science of treasures, logic, the science of ethics, etymology, the ancillary knowledge of the Vedas, the physical sciences, the science of war, the science of the stars, the science related to serpents, and the fine arts – all this I know, revered sir.'

VII-i-3: 'Revered sir, however, I am only a knower of verbal texts, not a knower of Atman. Indeed I have heard from persons like your revered self that a knower of Atman goes beyond grief. I am in such a state of grief. May your revered self take me across it.' Sanatkumara replied to him,' Whatsoever you have studied here, really it is only a name.'

VII-i-4: 'Name indeed is Rig-Veda, (so also) Yajur-Veda, Sama-Veda and the Atharvana as the fourth, the Itihasa-Purana as the fifth, grammar, the rules of the worship of the ancestors, mathematics, the science of portents, the science of treasures, logic, the science of ethics, etymology, the ancillary knowledge of the Vedas, the physical science, the science of war, the science of the stars, the science related to

> serpents, and the fine arts – name alone is all this. Worship the name.
>
> VII-i-5: 'He who worships name as Brahman becomes free to act as he wishes in the sphere within the reach of name, he who worships name as Brahman'. (Narada) 'Revered sir, is there anything greater than name ?' (Sanatkumara) 'Surely, there is something greater than name'. (Narada) 'Revered sir, communicate it to me.'

Chandogya Upanishad

Here, Sanatkumara asks Narada to describe what he already knows, so that Sanatkumara can take it from there. Narada describes his existing knowledge of the sciences, arts and language. Sanatkumara says that these are all merely objective study, a method of studying, classifying and labelling, which he dismissively refers to as 'the study of name'. You might know the names and purpose of every piece of equipment in the gym, but you will never get fit unless you actually use them. Beyond this external knowledge is subjective study, where one learns to not only understand, but subjectively experience the deeper mysteries

of life. This is the intellectual approach, of learning the theory and then going deeper.

Creative people, on the other hand, have something special about them. They have minds that are usually diffused and in a constant state of unease with the material world, living with an intuitive awareness of something beyond, without knowing what it is. It is only when they are expressing their creativity that their mind gets a razor sharp focus and they get lost in their activity. Such people have a natural inclination for spiritual life and find it easy to enter a meditative state of mind without understanding what they are doing, or why.

Either way, it is where the journey begins.

The following extract from the *Annapurna Upanishad* describes the state of mind of a seeker.

> II-27. Loving the Spirit, lifted above all hopes, full, holy in mind, having won the incomparable state of repose, he seeks nothing here.

> II-28. He is called the Jivanmukta (Liberated in life) who lives, unattached, in the pure Being that sustains all, the indubitable Spirit that is the Self.
> II-29. He craves not for what is yet to be; he does not bank on the present; he remembers not the past; yet he does all work.
> II-30. Ever unattached to those who cling to him; devoted to the devotees; he is harsh, as it were, to the harsh.
> II-31. A child amidst children; adult amidst adults; bold amidst the bold; a youth amidst the youthful; lamenting amidst those who lament;
> II-32. Steadfast, blissful, polished, of holy speech, wise, simple and sweet; never given to self-pity.

Annapurna Upanishad

This describes how a person should live a regular life, do what is expected of him, while maintaining a sense of detachment to whatever he is doing.

GURUS

There was a time when I could meditate all by myself, with no external aid, no tools, and no idols. I could meditate at any time, any place. Then I thought, why not use an aid to go further

than where I was? So I downloaded a couple of apps on my phone to help with breathing and timing, and they were certainly useful. But soon, I became dependant on these tools, and found that I could no longer meditate if I did not have my mobile phone handy, or if I was in an environment where I could not play the apps. I lost the ability to meditate at any time and any place.

Teachers, books, groups, idols, apps, etc are all tools to help you reach a certain level of understanding, but they can only help you go so far. They will not help in the actual awakening. You have to do that alone. Different tools have different purposes in your journey towards awakening, but as you go from one level of proficiency to another in your spiritual journey, you have to abandon all tools, including teachers, in favour of others more suited to the next step. At some point of time in your journey, they all becomes mere distractions and must be abandoned. When you reach the final stage where you are ready

to awaken, you will neither need nor have any external tools. You must do that all by yourself.

VI-30. (As novice) he shall be devoted to the welfare of his elders and reside a year there (in the abode of the Guru). He shall always be vigilant in the observance of the lesser vows (niyamas) as well as the great moral duties (yamas).

VI-31. Then at the end (of the year) having attained the excellent Yoga of wisdom he shall move about the country in conformity with (lit. without antagonizing) right conduct.

VI-32. Thereafter at the end of another year he shall give up (even) the excellent wisdom of the Yajnavalkya and the triad of orders (of Kutichaka, etc.,) and reach the state of the Paramahamsa.

VI-33. And bidding farewell to the Gurus (elders and preceptors) he shall indeed move about the country, giving up all attachment, subduing anger, being very moderate in diet, and conquering the senses.

Muktika Upanishad

Every teacher you learn from, every book you read (including this one), is nothing but a rung in the ladder that you must climb, a

guide in your journey, a sign-post on your path. Each one plays a specific and temporary role in guiding you on towards the next stage of your journey.

The *Upanishads* state that the material world is an illusion, and the notion of Guru and disciple is just another construct of this material world, something to be left behind in the search for enlightenment.

> III-52. The master and the disciple are unreal, the mantra of the Guru is unreal, that which is seen is unreal, but know me to be the Real.

Tejo-Bindu Upanishad

Even a God you worship is merely a stepping stone in your personal spiritual growth. You may choose to show respect or gratitude towards your gods and teachers, or you may choose not to. It is entirely up to you and will not affect your journey.

But under no circumstance must you interrupt your journey to stay back and remain in worship of any teacher. To stay back and worship a teacher is like worshipping a pointing finger.

"I would like to see the moon."
"Its right there, see?"
"I don't see it."
"That's because you are not looking at it."
"But I am looking at your finger, and your finger will show me the moon."
"My finger is already showing you the moon right now. Just look at the direction where it is pointing."
"No, I want to look at your finger. Your finger will show me the moon. All hail the Finger!"

Self

This advice is not about being respectful or disrespectful towards a Guru. The underlying principle behind respect for a Guru is that the Guru, like all other living beings, is no different from the inner self you are trying to seek. By worshipping the Guru as a separate entity, you are creating a duality that should not exist.

II-42. Thou, O Lord, art the partless non-dual essence (stated) in the books, in me, in Thee and in the ruler. He who thus perceives 'I' as of one homogeneity (pervading everywhere) will at once be emancipated through this spiritual wisdom. He is his own Guru with this profound spiritual wisdom.

> V-46. The whole universe is of the nature of Atman. All this is of the nature of Brahman. Asat is not of the nature of Brahman. There is not a grass different from Brahman. There is not a seat different from Brahman; there is not a Guru different from Brahman; there is nor a body different from Brahman. There is nothing different from Brahman like I-ness or you-ness.

Tejo-Bindu Upanishad

Ultimately you will become merged with your larger identity; you will become your own Guru. That inward journey is yours, and yours alone, and you must keep moving. Grab the next rung, abandon the previous one, and keep moving forward.

Desire

Desires play a very important role in a person's spiritual journey. Books on Hinduism have covered this subject in great depth. Human desire is natural, as is our tendency to fulfil them. Hinduism does not treat desires as sin. In fact, human desire is specifically acknowledged as a necessity. Desire is classified into four

main categories, each necessary for existence: *Dharma, Artha, Kama, Moksha.*

1. Dharma is the desire to live a morally healthy life in society, performing our duties and responsibilities towards ourselves, our family, and the world around us.
2. Artha is the desire for a materially fulfilling life. Wealth, income, prosperity.
3. Kama is the desire for an emotionally fulfilling life, including the desire for love, sex, happiness, and others.
4. Moksha is spiritual fulfilment, the desire to understand and transcend our worldly life.

When thoughts and desires become intense in a person, they go deeper than the mind and intellect to leave an imprint, known as *vasana,* on the consciousness. When this consciousness manifests itself in a new body after the death of the old one, it carries these imprints along with it.

This is an entirely non-judgemental process, where the nature of the vasanas do not matter.

Regardless of whether they are good imprints or negative ones, they get carried forward to the next birth. They do not affect where you will be born next, or in what kind of body, but they do determine the characteristics of the person you will be born as next. This is the principle of karma.

If you were a spiritual seeker in one birth, your consciousness will be more spiritually inclined in its next body, and that person will in turn have an even more intense spiritual desire in life. Similarly, if a person faces extreme financial worries and is always thinking of ways to make money, the next manifestation of his consciousness will be as a person who is single-mindedly focussed on making money, perhaps from an early age. Whether he makes money through straight or crooked means is entirely his own free will.

Think of all the people you know who were born into poor families, but displayed an inclination for making money right from childhood and went on to become successful

businesspersons later in life. Think of all the people who have shown an inclination towards music from an early age.

This phenomenon is especially prominent among artists, musicians, scientists and other creative people, who are naturally given to working intuitively, rather than by conscious brain-storming, in their respective fields.

> On 2 September, he [physicist Freeman Dyson] boarded a bus bound for the East Coast. 'On the third day of the journey a remarkable thing happened,' he wrote to his parents a few weeks later. 'Going into a sort of semi-stupor as one does after 48 hours of bus-riding. I began to think very hard about physics, and particularly about the rival radiation theories of Schwinger and Feynman. Gradually my thoughts grew more coherent, and before I knew where I was, I had solved the problem that had been in the back of my mind all this year, which was to prove the equivalence of the two theories.'

Drawing Theories Apart: The Dispersion of Feynman Diagrams in Postwar Physics by David Kaiser

Vasanas are different from memories. Memories are a biological phenomenon, a product of the

neurons and their interconnections within the brain. Memories die with the physical body and do not transmigrate with consciousness. Vasanas, on the other hand, are deep imprints created on consciousness itself. They drive our intuitive and emotional responses to worldly events, which then go on to shape the rest of our lives. It is the cause of greed, ambition, lust, revenge, ego, and other such material desires. It leads to human restlessness, and a sense of attachment to possessions.

One man may see a wallet filled with money on the ground and take it home, while another man may see a similar wallet and try to return it to the owner. The difference between the two people, intuitively driven to display such different behaviours in an identical situation, is the result of the vasanas or primal tendencies that exist in their consciousness.

Desires are natural and one cannot overcome them by suppressing them. The moment the mind engages with the external world, it becomes a slave, and all positive and negative

emotions come into play. You now have two choices – you can either work hard to satisfy your desires, or grow larger than them so that they are no longer important to you.

You can measure your state of happiness as a ratio of the number of desires you have in total, to the number of desires you have fulfilled. You can increase this ratio by two ways – either by leading a materialistic life, that is by increasing the number of desires you had fulfilled, or by leading a spiritual life, by decreasing the total number of desires you hold.

To abandon desire is to free up the mind from thinking, for a brief while. It does not mean you should give up attachments and desires altogether, but only for the duration of the meditation session. For that duration, disengage your mind from the world, calm it, eliminating emotions, and thus become the master of your universe.

Think of it this way. Imagine you are at a gym, planning to lift a heavy weight that you have never lifted before. Before you start, you have

the enthusiasm. You are motivated by a desire to look good. You probably even imagine the rippling muscles you will get in the near future. But once you start, in that moment when you are actually lifting it, you are not thinking about any of these things. Your mind is completely blank, you are definitely not thinking about how you will look. You are not even entertaining the desire to lift that weight, you are just lifting it.

For that brief moment, it is just you, the weight and your effort, nothing else. You did not lose your desire, you definitely did not grow averse to it, you merely forgot about it, and put it out of your mind for that brief moment.

It is important to note that this is just for the duration of the meditation session. But over a period of time, as you grow in spirituality, you will automatically develop a disinterest in the things you once desired.

It is equally important to understand that, at least in the spiritual context, the opposite of attachment is indifference, not aversion.

Those who have grown in spirituality and risen above their attachments show neither attachment nor aversion, they are merely indifferent to it all.

For example, you may have had many toys to play with when you were a child, and you may have had serious fights with your friends over these toys. But when you grew older, these toys no longer meant anything to you. You remained friends with those you had fought with as a child. You did not suppress your desire for toys, you simply grew out of it. And so it will be for all your material desires as you grow along the spiritual path.

Sin

In spirituality, there are no sins, just a set of actions that might distract your concentration when you are sitting in meditation. Greed, anger, lust, pride, etc., these are all actions driven by desires. They are capable of destroying a person's mental focus, and distracting one from the path of discovering the true Self.

Actions, by themselves, have no moral value. It is the intent that matters. A good man prays; so do thieves. A soldier kills; so do murderers. In Hinduism, even gods who have discovered their inner consciousness, have been known to cross the line once in a while.

A sin is any activity that keeps you thinking about matters related to the material world and distracts you from your efforts to transcend it. Even spiritual concepts cause you to think more about the concepts than focussing on the act of meditation. It is better to deal with such thoughts and activities first, to your satisfaction, before proceeding with meditation.

This idea is represented by the non-judgemental word 'karma' in Hindu philosophy, where, unlike most other religions, there is no concept of good and evil, only material and spiritual. From this perspective, unnecessary debates are counter-productive. Intense debates serve no purpose, so it is best to avoid people who argue more than is necessary. The only spiritually productive discussion is one where a

teacher provides guidance to a genuine seeker. Having achieved the enlightened state, you will in any case lose the desire to convince and impress others through debate. You will find it preferable and more productive to teach those who approach you with an open mind.

By the same token, enjoying a healthy appetite is not a sin, but overindulgence in food can become one, causing health problems that interfere with your spiritual progress. Even a cough or joint pain can become an impediment. It is the same with sexuality. It is not a sin in itself, unless sexual thoughts distract your mind while meditating, or your lover's spouse comes knocking on your door while you are in meditation.

Dishonesty is by itself not a sin either. But after advancing along the spiritual path, you automatically develop a heightened sense of integrity, not out of altruism, but because you no longer care for any material gains that can be had through dishonesty. You no longer consider it worth the effort. You develop a casual sense of recklessness, where you no

longer worry about the adverse consequences of honesty. You consider yourself so far beyond the material world that your attitude becomes, 'Just tell the truth. What's the worst that can happen?' To this extent, a spiritually advanced person inherently becomes an honest person.

> IV-9. He who knows this thus, with his sins destroyed, becomes firmly seated in the infinite, blissful and supreme Brahman. He becomes firmly seated (in Brahman).

Kena Upanishad

In summary, Hindu philosophy states that sin is anything that keeps us from discovering our higher consciousness.

6 MEDITATION

MEDITATION IS THE PROCESS BY WHICH a person can discover their true Self. There is a difference between knowing about Brahmaan and knowing Brahmaan. Spirituality is knowing about it, while meditation is the process of knowing Brahmaan, of becoming one with it. You can theorise that it exists. You can believe that it exists. You can even be convinced that it does. But to know it subjectively, you need to experience it for yourself.

When you meditate, you are going beyond the concept of God. You are reaching out to your inner Self.

According to Hindu philosophy, your true Self is beyond your thoughts. You can identify with your Self only when the thoughts in your mind have died down. Meditation is the process of making that happen. This requires stillness of mind, which is a big challenge. Meditation provides a set of techniques for babysitting the

mind, treating it like a child, and changing its behavioural patterns, until you have it firmly under your control.

The biological science behind meditation, and specifically its impact on the brain, is quite straightforward. The brain is made of neurons, which are cells that form the basic building blocks of the brain and the rest of the nervous system. These neurons have thin branch-like filaments called dendrites and axons, extending out of them, and neurons use these filaments to communicate with each other. Typically, a connection is formed between two neurons when the dendrites of one neuron joins with the axon of the other to form what is called a synapse. These synapses are what form memories and associations in the brain, and our thoughts are merely electrical impulses travelling from neuron to neuron via these synapses.

The interesting thing is that these synapses are like muscles. If used often, they get stronger, and that memory becomes long lasting. But if

not used often, they become weaker over time until they break entirely. This is why repetition leads to better memorisation. If you meet a person often, you remember their names and faces much better because the neural connections associated with that person have become strong. On the other hand, if you meet a person after a long time, the corresponding synapses will have weakened or broken down, so you may have difficulty in remembering the name, or even the person.

Similarly, emotion is the other factor that drives neural learning. Fear, for example, strengthens our survival instincts. A major tragedy, a first romance, a terrible humiliation, are all highly emotional events that you remember for a long time, perhaps all your life. This is why the mind gets distracted during meditation. It traverses pre-established connections, jumping from one thought to another. These are the inner, self-generated distractions.

Then there are the external distractions, each connecting to the next. While meditating,

you are disturbed by raised voices in the neighbouring house, you think about going to a temple, which reminds you that the car's fuel tank is empty, which then reminds you that your friend did not fill it up after borrowing it, and then you spend the next few minutes of your meditation time cursing your friend.

The *Upanishads* refer to this behaviour as the monkey-like mind.

> III-5. Then he, with his sinless mind, (reflected on) the (degree of) steadiness of his mind: 'clearly, though withdrawn, this mind of mine is extremely restless'.
>
> III-6. It wanders from a cloth to a pot and thence to a big cart. The mind wanders among objects as a monkey does from tree to tree.

Annapurna Upanishad

The aim of mantra-based meditation and other variants is to weaken these links and strengthen a single channel that will keep the mind focussed in any one direction. Meditation literally rewires the brain.

Your mind is the gateway to the larger universe, but as long as your consciousness is lost among thoughts, you will never be able to discover it. The final stages of meditation involve techniques to break that last single channel, so that ultimately there are no thoughts at all in the mind, and you can withdraw your consciousness beyond the mind and thoughts, into the larger universe.

This is beautifully illustrated in the *Mahaprasthanika* event, the Pandavas' final journey in the *Mahabharata*. The *mahaprasthan* means 'great journey', referring to the individual's inward journey of self discovery.

> The story is set 36 years after the epic battle. Krishna is dead, and Indraprastha is moving towards decadence. The guru Vyasa has advised the Pandavas that the time has come for them to retire from political life and seek spiritual advancement. Accepting his advice, the Pandava brothers install Parikshit as King of Indraprastha, and set out on their final journey. There were six of them, the five Pandava brothers and Draupadi, and later, a stray dog that joins them for some reason.

Along the way, as each of the Pandavas falls, one by one, this is symbolic of human spiritual process. Draupadi symbolises the human ego, and the five Pandavas represent the five senses wedded to this ego, in mutual enjoyment of material pleasure.

The first to fall is Draupadi (ego). In our spiritual journey, our ego is the first thing we must let go of.

The next to fall is Sahadeva, who represents intellectual arrogance, the tendency to think that you know it all and don't have anything more to learn. When this tendency falls away, you gain the humility to realise there is so much more to learn.

Next, Nakula falls. He represents physical vanity, the desire to look good. When you lose this tendency, you will no longer give undue importance, any more than is necessary, to physical appearance.

Then it is Arjuna who falls. He represents the arrogance of power, the belief that you can do anything you want, in the manner and time frame of your choosing. While self-confidence is always a good trait to have, this form of arrogance is counterproductive to the spiritual journey because it keeps you from rising above delays and failure.

Once you lose this arrogance, you will gain the humility to understand that if you haven't succeeded so far, it is only because you haven't put in the correct and/or sufficient amount of effort.

Then Bhima falls. He represents gluttony, not just of food, but of any form of material enjoyment. When we lose this tendency, we lose interest in material pleasures, and our desires fall off as a natural phase of our inner growth.

Finally Yudhisthira remains, along with the. Indra, God of the Senses, comes to tell him he can now enter heaven, that is, gain spiritual awakening, but on one condition: Get rid of the dog.

Yudhisthira refuses, arguing that the dog has been a constant companion and there is no way he will proceed without the dog. At this, the dog reveals himself to be Dharma, the human sense of duty, and Yudhisthira agrees to move forward alone.

The symbolism of Indira's appearance in this final stage is significant. Indra is also known as the God of the Senses (*indriyas*). He is depicted as a god who feels threatened whenever anyone is advancing on the spiritual path. He deliberately disturbs those on the verge of attaining enlightenment.

His appearance at this stage represents the idea that as a last resort, materialism (that is, sensory desires as represented by Indra), will use your sense of duty (dharma) to try and prevent you from progressing further. This is when you realise that to go forward you must abandon even your dharma, your duties. It is possible for you to gain control over every other tendency, but you will find it very difficult to abandon your attachment and sense of duty towards your family, your fellow humans and so on.

But even that must necessarily happen. It does not mean you need to physically abandon everyone and everything and become a monk. It simply means you cannot proceed beyond a certain point in your spiritual evolution as long as you remain emotionally attached to these factors.

Self

Meditation techniques are used to navigate the inner space within your mind, to reach your divine identity. It requires attention and focus. It requires silence. You may go through many other methods of meditation initially, all of which serve different purposes. But the ultimate meditation you will perform is silent

meditation, having silenced both the body and the mind. It is what will guide you to your destination.

One constant thought during the meditation process is that you must strive to withdraw into yourself, and then grow larger into divinity. You are like a drop of water that first squeezes through a tiny hole, then falls into an ocean and finally becomes an indistinguishable part of that ocean. You keep withdrawing into yourself, becoming smaller and smaller, until you identify with your consciousness. The moment you reach there, your consciousness expands into the larger four-dimensional universe and you realise you are divinity. You become that divinity. In meditation, you want to grow into your divinity, not reduce it down to your level.

The stages of awakening are described in the *Upanishads* as follows:

> III-15. As a bird, for flying in the sky, leaves the net (in which it was enmeshed), the great sage sheds (his) identification with the sense- organs;

then (he sheds) his awareness of limbs which has become illusory.

III-16. He has won the knowledge of a new-born infant; as if the air should give up its power to vibrate, he has terminated the proneness of consciousness to attach itself to objects.

III-17. Then, attaining the unqualified state of Consciousness – the state of pure Being – resorting, (as it were), to the state of dreamless slumber, he has stayed immovable like a mountain.

III-18. Winning the stability of dreamless sleep he has attained the Fourth; though gone beyond bliss, (he is) still blissful; he has become both being and non-being.

III-19. Then he becomes that which is beyond even the range of words which is the nihil of the nihilist and Brahman of the knowers of Brahman

Annapurna Upanishad

The final stage is known as *samadhi.*

Now I will tell you about Samadhi (deep meditative state) which destroys the ills of birth and death. Samadhi is that state in which there is knowledge that Jeevatma and Paramatma are one.

> Atma (soul) is filled all over for ever and does not have motion or stain. Though it is one, due to the effects of illusion, it appears as different objects. Really there is no difference between these so called objects. When one sees all objects within himself and him as a part of all objects, He attains Brahman.

Jabala Darsana Upanishad

As a meditator, you are like a white-water rafter... the material world is the powerful river that takes you forward at a deadly speed. You have some level of control over your direction, but only to the extent that you can avoid rocks and other dangers. Your goal is to break free entirely.

Forms Of Meditation

A pure spiritual way of life is not equally easy for everyone. It is easy for a *sanyasi,* an ascetic, who has given up worldly responsibilities and duties and spends most of his time in spiritual activities. On the other hand, it is usually difficult for a family person, who has various responsibilities and roles as parent, spouse, sibling and child.

Hinduism defines four different forms of meditation, each of which can be applied based on the individual's aptitude and circumstances. They are: *Karma Yoga, Bhakti Yoga, Jnana Yoga* and *Raja Yoga*. These forms are not mutually exclusive and the average person undertakes a combination of one or more forms in varying degrees. Moreover, they are not religious prescriptions, but a classification of normal human behaviour, based on observation.

- Bhakti Yoga is the path of worship, what most religions in the world today practise. What Hinduism calls Brahmaan is what they call heaven, and what they call hell is this very material world into which they are reborn repeatedly.

  The God they pray to is a human being who has transcended this material world to gain enlightenment. This yoga is for people who cannot understand the deeper aspects of spiritualism. A person praying at a temple or any other place of worship is implicitly performing Bhakti Yoga.

The key principle here is to worship your God with all your heart, and not be distracted by other thoughts. To follow the guidelines set out in your scriptures with complete sincerity.

- Karma Yoga is the path of action. It covers people who have worldly duties, such as the day-to-day work associated with earning a living and supporting a family. It also covers selfless work, such as social volunteers, NGOs, etc.

  Whether you're an office-goer, homemaker, or business person, there are responsibilities you have to deal with, and the key principle here is to perform your duties with all due concentration, without letting selfishness, worry, greed or ego enter the picture. Whether it is writing software, closing a deal, doing the dishes or preparing a report, the goal is to act without expectation of results, keeping the mind focussed on the task at hand.

- Jnana Yoga is the path of knowledge, and covers intellectual people; those who think

critically and cannot accept anything purely on blind faith. This path includes teachers, scientists, philosophers, thinkers and even atheists. These are people who use their intellect to expand human knowledge and seek to improve the human quality of life as a result. The guiding principle here is learning from various sources, with an open mind, with the intention of gaining the understanding and knowledge to undertake the inward journey.

- Raja Yoga is the path of meditation. It covers people who are mentally capable, and practically in a position to put their worldly duties and responsibilities on hold for a while. These are people who turn inwards and introspect to discover their inner identity. This group covers mystics, and introspective religions such as Buddhism, Jainism and Taoism.

Raja Yoga and Jnana Yoga are the two paths we will concentrate on in this book. As mentioned above, these paths are not mutually exclusive.

We usually walk one or more of them in varying proportions during our lives. For example, a salaried worker goes to a temple – that is a combination of Karma Yoga and Bhakti Yoga.

Sometimes these proportions change during the lifetime of an individual. For example, you can progress from extreme devotion to deep introspection at some point in life.

A person who is fundamentally non-conscious cannot achieve enlightenment. The best he can hope for is Bhakti Yoga. Some people may be able to reach enlightenment with minimal guidance and effort, while others may spend their entire lives leading a spiritual existence and still not get there.

TECHNIQUES

There are various meditation techniques, each suitable for specific situations. Some apply when you are stressed, others when you are facing too many mental distractions, and yet others when you are ill, and so on and so forth. You may have one specific method that works

for you, or you may have a set of techniques you regularly choose between. Either way is acceptable, and it is okay to believe your method is the best, as long as you do not force others to accept it.

What we are most interested in are the techniques that help you to reach within and discover your true identity. Meditation is a process to help your inward journey, and this process is all about listening to your body, mind and soul. There is a lot to hear and feel if the seeker is willing. It is not a process of subduing the mind and sense organs, but bringing them under the control of your intellect, of turning them towards your goal in life – spiritual enlightenment. Trying to forcefully suppress anything, be it emotions, thoughts, fantasies or physical discomfort, will not work and probably only make it stronger through obsessive focus.

This process is about withdrawing your consciousness backwards into yourself, not about focussing your consciousness ahead of

you onto something that can be observed. Imagine your consciousness as awareness of the world you observe. Imagine it disassociating itself from that world, then detaching from the sense organs that perceive that world, and finally depersonalising itself from you and moving further inwards.

It is difficult to explain the idea of withdrawing the consciousness, and the best example I can think of is, when you have your hand in a bucket of water and want to remove it, you do not wonder where your hand should go, you don't wonder whether you should move it forward, to the left, right, up or down. You withdraw your hand, pulling it closer towards yourself.

Similarly, right now, your consciousness is out there, all over the place. You are seeing, hearing, feeling, etc. When meditating, do not wonder which direction your consciousness should go. Instead, imagine pulling it closer towards yourself. Withdraw it from your awareness of your surroundings, then withdraw it from your very thoughts, into the stillness of your Self.

You can rediscover your inner self only if you have a completely calm mind. The moment you undertake any action, think any thought, your mind gets thrown to the mercy of the material world. When your mind is calm, when you are doing nothing, thinking nothing, you are the absolute master of your awareness. Then you can make your consciousness go where you want it to go.

Do not think too much about anything that doesn't appeal to your common sense. There are no rules or prescriptions on how to meditate, and as such, everything suggested below are merely common sense guidelines, open to interpretation.

The first step is to find a quiet place, in your home, at a nearby temple or any other place of worship, a park, the riverside, even a burning ghat; any place where you will not be disturbed.

In this context, Hindu temples were originally designed to be conducive for meditation. They have historically been places for people to meditate and were built with the purpose

of helping humans rediscover their superconsciousness in a conducive atmosphere free from noise and disturbance. This is perhaps difficult to imagine when visiting some of the crowded and noisy temples today. Temples were usually designed as a symbolic reminder of the human condition. The idol is there for those who want a symbol to focus their attention on, but people go around the idol one or three times before actually seeing and worshipping it. This is symbolic of the difficulty people face before actually getting a vision of the divinity within themselves. The outside of the temples have intricate carvings, with some even having erotic sculptures. This again is symbolic – of the distractions seekers must get past before gaining entry.

So if you have a temple in your vicinity you can opt to go there, especially at times when there are fewer people. Sometimes, even a ceiling fan can be a disturbance, as are humidity or cold, so find a comfortable spot. Keep in mind that you should not get too attached to the place.

If it no longer gives you the solitude you need, be prepared to move on and find another. You could even identify more than one such place and switch between them on different days. For example, if your home has distractions during the day, you could meditate at the temple, and if the temple has crowds during the evenings, you could meditate at home. Or you could change locations just to break the monotony.

The place does not matter. The only thing that matters is that you have a distraction-free environment and a level of comfort. There is no particular posture that is better than others. You can sit, stand, walk or lie down. Anything is fine as long as you are comfortable.

Having got into a comfortable place and posture, your goal now is to calm your mind, silence your thoughts and focus your attention.

One way to start the process is by concentrating on your breath. Keep your attention on your breath, breathing deeply, using the stomach rather than the chest. The primary reason this

helps is conscious heavy breathing leads to increased oxygen flow to the brain. Second, by concentrating on breathing, we are focussing our attention on that one activity, excluding everything else. Remember to breathe consciously, keeping your conscious thought focussed on your breath, to the exclusion of all other thoughts.

This helps in getting rid of all distracting thoughts from the mind, at least for the brief duration you are sitting in meditation. It also helps to set a rhythm.

In the final stages you will feel your existing consciousness expanding and contracting to that rhythm before breaking through to expand and merge with higher consciousness in the four-dimensional universe.

Your next step is mantra meditation. The reason for this is that chanting a mantra helps to get rid of distracting thoughts from the mind for the duration of the meditation session. There is no spiritual importance to how beautifully a mantra has been rendered or sung. For a seeker,

a mantra is important to establish a steady rhythm to meditation.

Further, note that while mantras are important, they have no inherent potency in themselves. Notwithstanding anything you may read about 'powerful mantras', they are just sounds, and have no special powers. There is no meditation or mantra that will help get rid of whatever problems are stressing you out. You will still need to deal with them yourself after your meditation session is over.

At the same time, there is no point thinking about those problems for the next 30 minutes or so, especially if there is nothing you can do about them right now. You might as well put them aside and concentrate on your meditation. So the only importance of a mantra in a person's spiritual journey is that it helps to focus the mind. By repeating the mantra, you are clearing out all other thoughts and focussing your mind on just that one thought, the mantra.

Most mantras ask for *shanti* (peace). They are referring to internal peace, asking the mind to

be at peace. It is a prayer to yourself that says please don't think about material distractions while mediating. When you say Shanti, shanti, shanti...it's like saying to yourself, 'Silence, silence, silence...

You can choose any mantra that appeals to you. For example, *Soham, Om,* or *Om Namah Shivaya.* Choose one that is easy on the mind and comfortable to repeat. Keep it minimal and simple. You may want to use a bead necklace to count your repetitions. A typical Hindu *japamala* has 108 beads, with one slightly bigger than the others. This is so you will know by feel when you have completed one round of 108 without having to keep count.

After mantra meditation, your next step is to transition into silent meditation. Here you try to silence all the thoughts in your mind, including the mantra. In the context of meditation, thoughts are a result of your conscious mind wandering about the neural pathways in your brain. I say in the context of meditation because there is nothing intrinsically

bad about thoughts. They are important and necessary at all other times in our lives. It is only when you sit down to meditate that you should try to turn them off.

Here, silence refers to the mind's state. This is where you consciously try to keep the mind in a state of absolute stillness. This is, of course, easier said than done. When you are in silent meditation, you will get all kinds of distractions. The mind is constantly on so many things – past memories, the future, desires, fantasies, worries, unsolicited thoughts, tempting thoughts, random images, erotic fantasies. You will observe that the mind is like a small child, it always finds a way to slip away from the stillness.

There are many strategies available to help you deal with a restless mind, too many, in fact, to list here. For example, imagine your head is like a bowl of water, where every thought causes a vibration. Your goal is to try and keep the water as still as possible.

Another approach is to make your distractions meditate along with you. Is your meditation

getting derailed too often by thoughts of that horrible boss or attractive colleague? Imagine them sitting next to you and meditating. Explain the reasons for meditation to them in your mind, which in effect, you are explaining to yourself. This will reinforce your own efforts.

A third approach is mindful meditation, where you act like a neutral third party, observing the thoughts in your own mind. Have you ever seen someone laughing loudly in a group, but if they notice that you are staring at them, they become self-conscious, and try to control themselves, and try to act dignified? It's the same with your mind. Keep staring at it long enough and it will start to behave itself. When you observe your thoughts, you are developing an awareness of your thoughts. You are detaching yourself from your thoughts and identifying with your consciousness. It's a way to step back and watch your thoughts pass by, like sitting in a window watching people and vehicles pass by.

One way to do it is to set a repeating timer on your smartphone for a short duration, say

every 30 seconds. You can now keep your mind focussed on any one thought or object, such as a mantra, your breath, or perhaps a candle or a statue. At this stage, your mind may start wandering. Whenever the timer goes off, note whatever you were thinking about. You become, in effect, an external observer of your mind. Do this long enough and you will automatically find yourself becoming a more self-aware person.

The good news is that there are no rules to follow here. If you get distracted by some thought, you can either stop it or let it play out to your satisfaction and then get back to your meditation. There is no one but you watching your thoughts. There is no one judging you, and no one deciding on your behalf that you have been a naughty person so you should not receive self-awareness. You are the only one in control of your journey.

You can do this as many times as it happens, as long as you make it a point to get your mind back on track every single time. You might find it useful to measure the length of time you can

go without physical distractions such as looking up or responding to a noise or movement.

Think of your mind as a top spinning on a table. If you give the table a gentle nudge, the top will wobble for a bit and then re-center itself. If you give the table a hard shove, the top will fall over. But you can always pick it up and spin it again. No matter how many times this happens, the top will spin again the next time. In time, your mind will get used to the idea of staying still for longer durations.

While there is no one single technique that is better than the others, I would recommend Vipassana meditation. It is a meditative technique that uses breath in place of a mantra as the focal point for the mind. It is a residential course, usually 10 days in duration. It provides a safe and peaceful environment, away from the rest of the world, even to the extent of taking away your phones and screening all your incoming phone calls for genuine emergencies. It is an excellent option if you are looking for distraction-free guided meditation.

The *Chandogya Upanishad* describes the process of quietening the mind as follows:

> VI-viii-2: 'Just as a bird tied to a string, after flying in various directions and finding no resting place elsewhere, takes refuge at the very place where to it is tied, even so, dear boy, that mind, after flying in various directions and finding no resting place elsewhere, takes refuge in Prana alone; for the mind, dear boy, is tied to Prana.

Chandogya Upanishad

Over time, you will be able to establish a pattern. For example, two minutes breathing, two minutes chanting, two minutes observing the mind, one minute mental silence. There is nothing special about the order, timings or the ratio given above. It is an example. Just start the process and find a pattern that works best for you. Create your own style.

Imagine yourself as a beginner, learning to drive a car, venturing out into the streets for the first time. You are aware of everything around you – the other cars near to you, how fast they are moving, in which direction. You are also very

conscious about every action you make – how hard to press the accelerator, the brake, when to shift gears, etc. You are mentally calculating distances, estimating times, and so on. Your mind is fully focussed on every aspect of driving.

But, over time, as you get more experienced and confident, you stop consciously thinking about it. You reach a stage when you can drive a car intuitively. Your conscious mind wanders, you even think of other things while driving solely on instinct and muscle memory.

Similarly, after gaining sufficient experience, meditation will no longer require any ritual, specific time of day or place. It can be performed at any time, any number of times. You can do it multiple times during the day or you can skip it. You can enter the meditative state of mind while doing the dishes, travelling in a bus, or even watching TV. Distractions will be everywhere and your mind will deal with any immediate situation that comes along, but you will be trained to remain in a meditative state in the midst of distractions.

Time will now feel like it is passing more slowly. Every activity feels like it takes longer. Earlier, when you thought or worried about things, your mind would wander, and you would not realise the passage of time until you came back to reality. You would typically experience this when doing something by habit, such as the dishes, or showering, or even driving. This no longer happens when you become more mindful. You are conscious of every second that passes. You can go about your daily life, perform all your day-to-day activities, but your mind remains unattached and unaffected.

Progress Markers

During the course of meditation, you will have certain experiences that indicate you are making progress in your journey.

- You might experience a crackling sensation just above the throat, something like the breaking of a tree branch.
- You might hear a soft directionless sound in your head. This is *Anahata,* the unstruck

sound. This may be confused with tinnitus, but it is quite easy to differentiate between the two. Tinnitus is an irritating sound, and often the patient can identify the direction from which it originates. The Anahata, on the other hand, is mild and pleasant, like a buzzing or a waterfall. You will know it is Anahata if you ever feel its frequency changing while meditating. If you can hear it, you have reached a significant milestone. At this stage you can stop chanting, you can stop concentrating on calming the mind, and focus your attention on this sound. It will be with you all the time. Listen to it, let it guide you further in your journey. Let it take you to the next dimension.

- Another experience you may have is a shining, shimmering bluish patch that appears in your frontal and peripheral vision. It is usually oval in shape, with a jagged boundary, like a fractal pattern. When you experience it, you will realise it is not something you are seeing with your physical vision, you are sensing it in an inexplicable manner. To experience

something approximately similar, close your eyes and gently press on your eyelids, But it is obviously not the same thing. You will know the difference if you sense this shape on the outer edges of your peripheral vision, and perhaps even further back from there. Sometimes, instead of blue, you may see a fiery golden ring.

- You may experience a small sudden bright flash of white. It is not something you see with your eyes, but something you experience or sense, from any direction. For example, you might 'see' that white flash at the back of your head.
- You may experience sensations of movement, like you are moving, even though you are still. Like your consciousness is moving within you. This is somewhat similar to the experience of feeling dizzy, but much more pleasant.
- Yet another marker is a feeling like a gust of cool breeze in the centre of the skull.

- Sometimes, during a meditation session, you may experience a state of intense joy, an orgasm of the soul so to speak. You will feel hyperactive, experience an abundance of energy that makes you want to jump up and do something, but you don't know what. And at other times you will feel extremely dull and lethargic.
- Without warning you will feel like you are being pulled upward by your neck. Your chest expands, your eyes close automatically, your back straightens and then arches as an orgasmic shiver runs up and down your spine. You want to stay in this state as long as possible, but you snap out of it as suddenly as you entered it.

It is important to understand that you need not worry if you do not experience any of these things, or the order or sequence in which you experience them. Just keep yourself focussed on your meditation and let things happen as they will.

On a serious note, I generally try not to sound sensationalist in anything I say, but I must

address the issue of fear. Sometimes, when you have any of the experiences mentioned, it can be accompanied by a deep sense of foreboding or fear. This is the mind reacting in fear of the unknown. This is much deeper than merely our hesitation in making this attempt. This fear is real, similar to the fear you would feel if you were about to step off a cliff for the first time, even with a parachute and safety gear on. No matter how reassured you feel, your mind automatically rebels and your body automatically enters into survival mode. It is the fear of leaving the known and entering the unknown.

Just as evolution gave rise to the process of breathing as a life support mechanism, it also gave us the facility of conscious thought as another life support mechanism. And just as it is impossible for us to kill ourselves by holding our breath, it is impossible to transcend this universe by stopping our thoughts. The mind will simply not allow it. You are the end-result of centuries of evolution, of being outwardly

focussed for survival. The brain believes that not being outwardly focussed will result in certain death. It will automatically kick in, either with distracting thoughts of material benefits or worldly worries, or by generating a deep sense of fear of the unknown. This will be one of the greatest obstacles you will need to surmount in your journey.

This phenomenon is described in the *Upanishads* at many times. In some places, it is described as worldly distractions caused to the seeker by Indira, God of the Senses. At other places, it is presented as distractions caused by Yama, the God of Death. Just as Abrahamic religions personify evil as Satan or Shaitan, Hinduism personifies death. In this context, Death does not refer to the death of the physical body, but to the death of material existence, which takes place when a person surpasses the intellect and becomes enlightened.

The *Katha Upanishad* narrates the story of Nachiketa, who attempts to gain knowledge of the aatma. Yama has agreed to grant him

a boon, and Nachiketa asks Yama to give him the knowledge of what happens to one who goes beyond this world.

> I-I-20. This doubt as to what happens to a man after death – some say he is, and some others say he is not, – I shall know being taught by thee. Of the boons, this is the third boon.
> I-I-21. Even by the gods this doubt was entertained in days of yore. This topic, being subtle, is not easy to comprehend. Ask for some other boon, O Nachiketas. Don't press me; give up this (boon) for me. I-I-22. (Nachiketas said:) Since even by the gods was doubt entertained in this regard and (since) thou sayest, O Death, that this is not easily comprehended, no other preceptor like thee can be had to instruct on this nor is there any other boon equal to this.
> I-I-23. Ask for sons and grandsons who will live a hundred years. Ask for herds of cattle, elephants gold and horses, as also for a vast extent of earth and thysself live for as many autumns as thou desirest. I-I-24. If thou thinkest any other boon to be equal to this, ask for wealth and longevity. Be thou the ruler over a vast country, O Nachiketas; I shall make thee enjoy all thy longings.

> I-I-25. What all things there are in the human world which are desirable, but hard to win, pray for all those desirable things according to thy pleasure. Here are these damsels with the chariots and lutes, the like of whom can never be had by men. By them, given by me, get thy services rendered, O Nachiketas, do not ask about death.

Katha Upanishads - 1-I

Here, Yama tells Nachiketa to ask for something else, anything but such knowledge of death. But Nachiketa is adamant.

> I-I-26. These, O Death, are ephemeral and they tend to wear out the vigour of all the senses of man. Even the whole life is short indeed. Be thine alone the chariots; be thine the dance and music.
> I-I-27. Man cannot be satisfied with wealth. If we need wealth, we shall get it if we only see thee. We shall live until such time as thou wilt rule. But the boon to be asked for (by me) is that alone.
> I-I-28. Having gained contact with the undecaying and the immortal, what decaying mortal dwelling on the earth below who knows the higher goal, will delight in long life, after becoming aware of the (transitoriness of) beauty (Varian) and sport (rati) and the joy (pramoda) thereof.

> I-I-29. O Death, tell us of that, of the great Beyond, about which man entertain doubt. Nachiketas does not pray for any other boon than this which enters into the secret that is hidden.

Finally Yama relents.

> I-II-3. Thou hast relinquished, O Nachiketas, all objects of desire, dear and of covetable nature, pondering over their worthlessness. Thou hast not accepted the path of wealth in which perish many a mortal.
>
> I-II-4. What is known as ignorance and what is known as knowledge are highly opposed (to each other), and lead to different ways. I consider Nachiketas to be aspiring after knowledge, for desires, numerous though they be, did not tear thee away.

This story describes anthropomorphically, the process that takes place when a person gains awareness of his higher identity. Yama, the God of Death (that is, death of the material body), offers all kinds of temptations to Nachiketa, to dissuade him from proceeding. This is symbolic of how, even when we are on the verge of self-identification, the material world continues to distract us.

7 STORY

HERE ARE SOME SPIRITUALLY meaningful short stories. Through the entire course of human history, enlightened men and women have attempted to tell the world about the need for humans to discover themselves. And we have seen such messengers being persecuted by dogmatic people of religion in the past, and people of science in modern times. A spiritual seeker can safely ignore both and set forth on the journey.

THE MAN WHO COULD SEE

Janaka Island was nothing more than an isolated rock in the Andaman cluster, missed by centuries of explorers because of the permanent swirling mists and shallow waters that surrounded it. It was named after Dr. Janaki Menon, Head of the team that discovered it in 2001. The native villages were like any other tropical hamlets, with plenty of green cover and sunlight when it was not raining.

Sadly, the natives could not see the sunlight, or the sun for that matter. They were blind. They have been blind for as many generations as they could remember. They could no longer understand the concept of sight, nor did they have a word for vision in their vocabulary.

Over the years, this had become a society where sound and memory played a very important role in identifying people and places, or even in staying safe from reptiles. The villagers could detect the presence of snakes and crocodiles by sound, from 10 or even 15 steps away, which was a good enough for retreating or skirting around the creatures. The only time someone ever got killed by a crocodile was when it was hiding in water, because that was when it was silent.

Needless to say, Janaki was intrigued by these people. How did they come to lose their sight? But she was a geologist, not a doctor or anthropologist. She needed to take one of them back to get her answers. During her three-month stay, she had managed to pick up

a smattering of the language, helped by the fact that it had some similarities with her native Malayalam. She had struck up a good rapport with Emmei, a young boy in his late twenties, who tagged along with the team as they went about on short expeditions.

She was impressed by his curiosity and intelligence, while he simply couldn't understand how she could know about the presence of a crocodile from over 100 steps away. What did she mean she could 'see' them? He had heard folklore stories of ancient gods who could do that, but knowing the fear and suspicion it would invoke among his people, he was wise enough not to mention it to anyone.

Over time, she persuaded him to return to mainland India with her. She took him to the Govt. Medical College at Trivandrum, where he was attended by the best ophthalmologists in the country. They made a surprising discovery. He had a fully developed pair of eyes and optic nerves and everything else necessary for full vision. His 'blindness' was merely caused

by his eyelids getting sealed shut over the years. They could not tell how that came to be, but the surgery to reopen them was simple.

A few days later, the bandages came off. Emmei opened his eyes, and promptly fainted. His brain had become overwhelmed by the sensory overload, the doctors said. They replaced the bandages and planned to try again later. He refused to open his eyes. He kept his hands firmly over them. It took a team of doctors, counsellors and psychiatrists to persuade him over several days, before he took the next peek, and the next.

For a while, nothing made sense to him. A person was, to him, a disembodied sound and a rough shape in his mind that he would form by touch and feel. Now that shape took a more concrete form in his mind. He was able to know the shape of the person without touching. He once tried, in the spirit of science, to compare the mental image he had formed by touch with the image he got through his eyes. Sadly, the experiment failed when his subject, a shapely nurse, slapped his hand away.

But his other experiment was a success. He was able to walk using his newfound sense of sight. Earlier, he would walk on unfamiliar territory by slowly moving each leg forward, close to the ground, to check for any obstacles. Now he learned to step over them, knowing well in advance of their presence. It was an incredibly liberating feeling.

Over the weeks, the novelty wore off, both for him and the doctors. He was, for all purposes, a normal human being whose vision had been restored. Not a big deal for an ophthalmologist. And Emmei began yearning for home. Soon, the hospital administration started thinking of the room he was occupying for free and decided it was time to release him.

He was flown home in a Navy chopper, accompanied by Dr. Menon. It was a beautiful homecoming. Everyone embraced each other. The celebrations lasted two days. The doctor returned to the mainland. The celebrations finally ended and life returned to normal.

Emmei has not told anyone about his superpower yet. He didn't know how to bring it up or explain it. He feared how they would react. Once, when he was at a neighbour's house, the man was searching for his walking stick. "It's outside, near the pond," he said without thinking. The neighbour went out and returned with the stick, throwing him a suspicious look. Emmei realised what he had done and hurried from the house. It was time to start talking.

He began with magic tricks. "Put any object 10 steps in front of me and I'll tell you what it is," he said. "How did you guess?" they asked every time he answered correctly. He would occasionally give a wrong answer on purpose. He still did not know how they would react when things got serious, which it soon did.

There was a wedding in the next village. He could see it was a beautiful sunny morning and the villagers had gathered to set out together. "Don't go yet," said Emmei. "There's a crocodile in the river by the path." But he had

played his tricks so many times by then that they merely thought he was fooling around. Ten minutes later, they came running back, screaming and frightened.

And they were angry. Especially the village Headman, whose son had just been killed. "How did you know?" they asked Emmei. "What magic is this?" He replied, "I can know without touching." "Impossible!" they shouted. "Only the gods can know without touching!"

Despite the tragedy, Emmei smiled. He told them he was no god. What he could do, anyone could. With a little help from his new friends, he could help them and open up a whole new world to them. He could barely contain his excitement. "Just imagine the progress and development that can come to you," he said. The possibilities were endless.

It was just a little before noon on that bright sunny day when the villagers dragged him to a clearing in the forest and beat him to death.

The Man Who Held A Belief

"Open up!"

I was jolted awake by the loud and insistent knocking on the door of my dingy IBHK.

"Open up, I say!"

I dragged my sleepy self to the door and opened it to see three angry men, armed with pamphlets on evolution and quantum physics.

"Where is it, where is it?" they shouted as they pushed past me and entered my house. "We know you have it here somewhere."

"What exactly are you looking for?" I asked, perplexed.

"Your belief."

"My what?"

"Your belief! We know you have one here somewhere. We're here to rid you of it."

"But why?"

"They are dangerous things, you ignorant fool!"

"Really? Who are you guys, anyway?"

"We're scientists."

"Are you now? What streams of science are you from?"

"We're just scientists, you know, in general. We are fed up of being persecuted all the time by you people with beliefs"

"Who is persecuting you?"

"Er...well, no one per se. It's just..."

"Yes?"

"People kill each other because of beliefs! Today you believe in something, tomorrow you will be killing millions of people who disagree. And then what?"

"Oh come now...it's just a belief. Not that big a deal."

"Not a big deal? Do you have any proof of your belief??"

"No, it's just a belief..."

"How can you believe in something you have no proof of?"

"It's called a belief precisely because there is no proof."

Perplexed silence filled the room.

"You don't need to 'believe' the earth is round because it's a proven fact, right? You only 'believe' in something when there is no proof." I tried to help unclog their mental gears a bit.

It had the opposite effect. The perplexity levels intensified.

"Look," I said, "this is ridiculous! All I believe is..."

That seemed to un-perplex them into action.

"STOP! Stop it! Stop shoving your beliefs down our throats!"

"I wasn't. It was you who barged into my house demanding..."

"Shut up! Shut up! You're killing us with your beliefs. Stop this persecution!"

"Look, it's just..."

"La la la la la..."

I was beginning to get exasperated now. "Why are you here then?"

"We are here to educate you on the wonders of science. Do you know about science?"

"Yes, I imagine I do..."

"Be quiet! Don't you dare claim to know science. What would mass murderers like you know of science?"

I glanced at the not-flashing notification light on my cellphone and briefly rued my lack of followers on social media, much less followers for activities involving mass murder.

"I have a Bachelors degree in science, actually,"

"You do, do you? I suppose, next you'll be quoting quantum physics to support your beliefs?"

"Er. . .not really. . .I. . ."

"What is this nonsense belief of yours anyway?"

"Aliens"

Once again, silence filled the room. The perplexometer was off the charts now.

"Huh?"

"Aliens," I repeated. "I believe in the possibility of life on other planets."

They got into a huddle, with much urgent whispering and consulting of pop-science Youtube videos.

After a while, they turned back to me.

"Okay, we'll allow that."

"You will?"

"Yes, Neil The Grass Tyson has declared it is true."

"But…"

"And he's a scientist and all, so it has to be true."

"Not really. He merely said it's a possibility..."

"Heretic!"

I took a few quick steps back.

"How dare you! How dare you!" they chorused.

"But I thought you guys wanted proof, and there's no proof that…"

"Blasphemer!"

I ran and jumped behind the sofa, narrowly escaping a soft-cover copy of *A Brief History Of Time* as it flew past my head.

"Its DeGrasse, by the way," I told them.

They quickly reconfirmed this on Youtube before responding, "Be quiet, fool! Don't you dare take his name."

After I had been quiet for a while, they seemed to calm down. One of them said, "Since your belief is sciencey enough and has been approved by The Grass Tyson, we have decided to spare you."

"DeGrasse."

"Shaddup!"

I was truly relieved, not at being spared whatever inquisition they had planned for me

(which incidentally I would have preferred to their conversation), but simply because they were leaving. I could not resist one parting shot though.

"But what if aliens are, in fact, gods?" I asked slyly from behind the safety of my sofa.

My heart sank as they paused in their tracks, but it was momentary. They continued walking away.

"Oh the persecution..." I heard them mutter as they clattered down the stairs, away from my door. "Why do these people come after us with their beliefs like this? All this persecution will kill us one of these days..."

REFERENCES

Abbott Edwin Abbott. *Flatland*

Annapurna Upanishad

Bhagwad Gita

Brihadaranyaka Upanishad

Chandogya Upanishad

Jabala Darsana Upanishad

Kaiser David. *Drawing Theories Apart: The Dispersion of Feynman Diagrams in Postwar Physics*

Katha Upanishad

Kena Upanishad

Mandukya Upanishad

Muktika Upanishad

Mundaka Upanishad

Rig Veda

Sawmi Vivekananda. Speech at the Parliament of World's Religions 15 Sept. 1893

Srimad Bhagwatam

Swami Paramahansa Yogananda. *Autobiography of a Yogi*

Tejo-Bindu Upanishad

web page: *https://www.universetoday.com/38282/electron-cloud-model/*

Wikipedia

Yogi Gopi Krishna. *Kundalini: The Evolutionary Energy in Man*

Acknowledgements

MY SINCERE THANKS TO my friend Madhuri Joshi, for reviewing, proofreading and providing reader feedback on the manuscript.

My heartfelt thanks to Dr. Sunu Engineer, for reviewing the book, patiently correcting my mistakes, and successfully resisting the temptation to bonk me on the head with my own manuscript for my initially incorrect descriptions of some of the scientific and philosophical concepts.

Wish To Publish With Us?

We are always keen to look at interesting content across genres. Please email your submission to: **submissions@leadstartcorp.com**

The submission should include the following:

1. **Synopsis**
   A summary of the book in 500 – 1000 words. Please mention the word count of the manuscript.

2. **Sample chapters / Poetry**
   A couple of chapters from the book; these need not be in order, just send the best two chapters of the book. Or a few poems if the same is a collection of poetry.

3. **A Note About The Author**
   An interesting note about yourself (about 200 words).

4. **Additional Information**
   - Target audience
   - Unique selling proposition
   - List of illustrative content (if any)
   - Other comparative titles
   - Your thoughts on marketing the book